BRASS, BLIMPS AND BOTS

To Nar,

Merry Christmas 2022! Hope you
enjoy your trip aboard the
"Caeliner" ♡
Love,
Charlotte
x

Crystal Peake Publisher
www.crystalpeake.co.uk

First edition published in September 2022 by Crystal Peake Publisher

Print I S B N   978-1-912948-48-2
eBook I S B N   978-1-912948-49-9

A catalogue copy of this book is available from the British Library.

Typeset by Crystal Peake Publisher
Cover designed by Pete Heyes

Visit www.crystalpeake.co.uk for any further information.

BRASS, BLIMPS AND BOTS

Dedications

To my loving husband, who never stops believing in me.

N.J Mckay

To my wife Georgiene, who continues to support me and my wayward imagination...

Mark Piggott

To my family and friends for their never-ending support, and to every little girl who wanted to save the damsel.

Charlotte Byrne

To my steampunk gal and wife, Candy, and my treasure enthusiast father, Linton Sr.

Linton Valdock

Reviews are the most powerful tools for a publisher and an author. They help to gain attention for the books you enjoy reading. Honest reviews of our books helps to bring them to the attention of other readers.

If you have enjoyed this book, or any of our other books, we would be very grateful if you could spend just five minutes leaving a review. These reviews can be as short or as long as you like.

The Assassination of
Lady Carlyle
by ~~Charlotte Byrne~~

The Assassination of
Lady Carlyle
by Charlotte Byrne

It was dark in Governor Purbright's office. Vic squinted at the documents on her lap. She was trying to make out her target's particulars in the dim light from the oil lamp perched dangerously on the edge of the mahogany desk.

'What are "vose technics" when they're at home?'

Purbright squeezed the space between his eyes with his fingers. He often did this when Vic came out with these insufferable questions.

'"*Voce* technics", Miss Darnley. It comes from the Latin for "voice".'

'Voe-chi. Voe-*chay*.' She grimaced and crossed her legs. 'I'll go with "vose" if it's all the same to you, guv.'

'Go with what you will, but make sure he's *dead*.'

She nodded and continued reading the brief. Sir Arthur Dulcett was an eminent Academik and principal of The Dulcett Institute for Vocetechnical Research. His Sonophone had won numerous awards and had been an obscene success when it finally reached the commercial market. Morality, it seemed, was a grey area in high society. People were happy to give machines that played voices of their dearly departed as Christmas presents; even if it meant ripping out the voice boxes of those who were fresh in the ground in order for the moulds to be made. There were rumours circulating that they would offer animals next. It made Vic feel sick to wonder what they might have been experimenting with in the first place. The Queen herself was said to have a Sonophone that reproduced the voice of the late Prince Consort. She played it religiously before retiring to bed. You could programme what you wanted it to say simply by turning the dials in the back to different letters before winding it up, much like an automaton that actually wrote letters. Vic had once seen it at an exhibition. While that had been spooky, at least it didn't speak through a brass mask. That part of the Sonophone was a nightmare in itself, sitting on top of the box – it had moving lips that the sound came out of, and eye movements that were an optional extra for a few quid more. And while the Queen was fond of this fantastic invention, it seemed that she didn't care for its creator much if she wanted him dead.

'Just a few awards then,' Vic said, noting the list of accolades and prizes on the third page.

She worked her way through the documents quickly, pausing only to mull over the reproduced engraving of her target. It was a precise reproduction of the original daguerreotype, as good as the original itself. *A chilling face to match his work,* she thought. His deep-set eyes stared back at her from the paper, piercing through the shadows cast by the oil lamp. They danced across his face as the light flickered. Everything about him gave the impression that a skeleton had been dressed up, right down to the swallow-tailed beard that only accentuated his gaunt features. He was holding a Sonophone in his hands, the mask of the poor unfortunate resembling a devil.

'Funny sort of bloke, isn't he? This Dulcett.'

'You're not wrong,' Purbright scoffed, knocking back a tot of something brown.

That was the thing with the Force. There was always a good chance they were three sheets to the wind while on the clock. It was no wonder that the crime rate was higher than ever. Vic took one last look at the engraving's eyes and shivered before turning the page. Attached to the next page was a postcard with another engraving on it. An elaborate typesetting read 'LADY

SAPPHIRE CARLYLE as GILDA'. The young woman in the muslin dress was a welcome relief to the skeletal Dulcett.

'Ah!' Purbright piped up and put away the bottle. 'Now, this is the young lady you're to protect.' He had that bloody awful look on his face that told Vic the job she was bound for would be one he was glad *he* wasn't lumbered with. She frowned.

'Protect? I thought I just had to kill Dulcett?'

Purbright stood up and scratched one of his mutton chops before putting his hands behind his back.

'Yes, but it's sort of a... counter-assassination.'

Vic's head hurt just trying to process Purbright's words. A counter-assassination was counter-intuitive. You can't know when someone's about to be assassinated. That was the whole point of an assassination, wasn't it? The element of surprise, and all that rubbish. And how can an assassination be countered? Did both parties end up dead, or was it just one of them? In that case it would be a straightforward assassination, no countering because the poor bloke doing so would be dead.

'Sorry, guv, I'm not following you.'

Purbright sighed and leaned against the shelves that held twenty years' worth of his paperwork.

'Dulcett's going to kill her, so do him in before he gets the chance to! Lawks, Darnley, it's not hard!'

Vic smirked, pleased at still being able to rub him up the wrong way after four years of service.

'So you've had a tip, then?' She grinned. 'Why didn't you say so?'

Purbright's groan was more impressive than usual.

'Lady Carlyle is the world's leading soprano. Surely you can understand why Dulcett would want that voice?'

'Oh, the penny dropped,' said Vic, and looked a while longer on the engraving.

It would be a terrible waste to kill the woman for profit. She was beautiful. And, if all went Dulcett's way, the Sonophone could well end up putting an end to live music for good. The nails in the coffin were in place – they were just waiting for one final hammering.

'She is a pretty thing, though.'

Purbright rubbed at his temple.

'Please don't have any more of your wild ideas, Miss Darnley. If I have just one more young woman in here swearing blind you said you'd marry them, I shall jump into the Thames!'

Vic stood up, and tucked the folder into the slit she'd cut in the lining of her coat especially for storing big, flattish objects.

'It's all right, guv,' she said. 'I never flirt on the job.'

*

The tracked omnibus that went from the Bank of England and into the heart of Limehouse had only one other passenger besides Vic. It was an old woman in a shawl who kept banging on the ceiling with her cane. She was calling to the operator to take the brake off and angrily boasting how she could piddle faster than they were moving. She reminded Vic of her Nan. Still, when the old girl alighted at Shadwell, Vic was glad of the peace and settled back into her seat, enjoying the warm air that was pumped in through the ornate vents under the window. The conductor came down into the passenger's area a few minutes later, clapping his hands together and blowing into them. His cloak was damp, and he nearly slipped on the last step.

'Cold night, lad,' he said.

'I don't doubt it,' said Vic.

She didn't bother to correct the conductor. People generally assumed that she was a young man, either because of her hair, which she wore clipped close to her skin on the sides, or because of her preference for wearing trousers. Women generally only wore trousers while travelling or if they worked in any of the Services. In her line of work, it was always better not to draw attention. She put her feet up on the seat in front and stared out of the window. The snow had started to fall when she was still in her briefing and was now beginning to settle. It dusted the road, melting only in the grooves of the tracks, which were always hot. The pavements were covered in a light powder. There were a few people out and about who had either buried themselves in their coat collars or shawls, or had parasols up. The cranes and boats lining the river were lit up by gaslights; the taller ones had red glass lanterns at the top as a warning for airborne vehicles. Piercing through the darkness and the snow, they looked like macabre Christmas decorations.

'Limehouse – all change, please!'

The conductor didn't have to shout it, because it was only Vic aboard, but that was the protocol, and it had to be observed. She nodded at him as she alighted and headed for The Queen's Gubbins. The cold stung her ears and face, and she pulled up the collar of her coat. It didn't much matter. Tomorrow, she was on the first ship bound for Somaliland, where Lady Carlyle was to perform for the Sultans and the English dignitaries in a week's time. Whatever would happen over there, at least it would be warm.

The Assassination of Lady Carlyle

The late Lord Emmett Carlyle would never have allowed her out of the country alone, let alone go to Somaliland. That much Sapphire knew. She didn't want to look at the drab portrait that hung at the foot of her bed while she packed. It stared too hard at the best of times and appeared to narrow its eyes at her whenever anything remotely daring crossed her mind. A sprinkling of dust hung in the air as she turned it to face the wall. Then she wound up the reproductogram that sat on her dressing table and waited for the twenty-sixth movement of Handel's Messiah to come piping through the holes at the side. The poor thing was getting old and sometimes needed a good thump to get it going. Today was one such time, and after two strikes the music trickled through.

It wasn't that she needed the money, she thought as she brought out the trunk from under the bed, although that would be most helpful. It was that she simply needed to escape London. The lavish apartment she shared with Emmett before he died had become insufferable. (In went her collection of first editions). So, too, were the theatres she performed in, and the music halls that she was being booked in more and more frequently. That part was good. The working classes should be able to experience a little culture once in a while. After all, weren't they the majority of the population? (Gloves.) And didn't the country run on their unending labour? They, more than anyone, deserved to enjoy themselves. But even offering her gift towards that was not enough to tip the scale against the terrible weight that held her down. (She thrust in her petticoats.) Everywhere she looked she was reminded of Emmett, and, consequently, all that he had done to her. It wasn't just the torment, but being married to him was only marginally better than a three-year spell at Her Majesty's Pleasure. The food was better, and sometimes he bought her a nice gown just because she made a dying man so very happy. Generally, though, she hadn't had to make up her mind about anything in the five years they'd known one another. She'd gone straight from her mother's care into his at only sixteen. It was the done thing. (Three dresses would do, they'd provide the costumes.)

Well, no more, she thought happily, slamming the lid of the trunk. Three years she'd put up with him until he joined his family in the mausoleum. It had taken Sapphire only an instant to accept the Embassy's invitation when it arrived the October morning they interred him. She'd be out of the country for Christmas, of course, but that wasn't all that bad, was it? At least she wouldn't have to endure another tedious time with her family. It was bound to be worse this year, what with him gone. All reminiscing, and awful presents, drink flowing, and arguments started by Aunt Gladys because she should have married someone in the business, not nobility. And then there were the distant cousins who came only out of duty, but would otherwise not be seen dead with her. She could see their disapproving glares now.

Somaliland was *freedom*. It was doing things on her own terms. She could perform where she wanted, go where she pleased, and all without an escort. It would be an adventure, of sorts, although hardly as exciting as those in the books she loved so much. Nobody would stop her from living the way she wanted for the next few weeks. She checked once, twice, three times for her Caeliner ticket in her handbag, and then rang the bell on the wall. She'd make sure to leave the maids a few pounds so they could enjoy themselves, too.

* * *

There were nicer places to drink than The Queen's Gubbins, but they just didn't have that sense of home. Besides, it was the closest pub to the docks where her brother's ship was berthed for the next few days, and so it was the easiest place for them to meet.

Reggie looked different every time Vic saw him. People in the Services didn't tend to change their appearance much, but Reggie never did like sticking to the rules, even when they were younger. The last time they met he had a long beard that had got him a warning because it was against regulations. They didn't much mind when they were at sea, but on land they were representing the Queen's Navy and had to look the part. Tonight, waving her over through the smoke and noise, he looked more respectable in his favourite civvies – a collarless shirt; the sleeves rolled to show off his tattoos, and work trousers held up by scarlet braces – and he was clean shaven, with his hair and sideburns cropped short. Vic squeezed past some Gubbins' regulars to his table in the corner where he stood and folded her up in a hug.

'You got my bird then?'

Vic nodded and lowered herself onto the stool opposite him. The pigeon arrived a day before the ship docked.

'It's not half good to see you, Reg. How much leave have they give you?'

'We sail tomorrow.'

'Funny, so do I.'

Two glass tankards of cheap beer were delivered to the table through the hole in the wall. There was a hole at every table lining the walls, and you only had to pull a lever – once for 'same again', twice for 'service' if you wanted to change your order, or have a word with the landlord in the other room. The latter wasn't used much, mainly because the landlord didn't like to be disturbed, and he was known to gob in your glass if you gave him too much mouth. Vic knew this from experience and was glad that Reggie had already got them in. He slid hers over to her with one experienced push, and she'd downed half of it before he had time to ask her:

'Where are they sending you this time?'

'Somaliland.' She let out a belch and grinned with the satisfaction of making the people at the next table over look. 'I'll be gone for two weeks, I shouldn't wonder.'

Reggie considered this, sitting back in his seat and folding his arms over his chest.

'For one hit?'

'Yeah, well, the Caeliner's still a bit quicker than your floating tin.'

He laughed and started to reel off the reasons he'd take the sea over the air any day. She continued to nurse her drink, running her thumb over the tankard's handle. The player piano in the other corner began to hammer out a happy old tune that everyone in the place felt obliged to sing along with. Vic didn't know all the words. It all got a bit confusing in the third verse, after they'd mocked the spivs and moved on to the dandies. Reggie took the opportunity to kick a haversack to her under the table. It hit the foot of her stool with a metallic *clunk*, barely audible in the half-cut din.

'You're a bloody marvel,' she said, beaming. 'Is that... *it*?'

'Yeah. The captain owed me a favour – told me to help myself.'

'Cor. You ought to do him more favours.'

She leaned forward to grab the bag, but Reg's boot crunched her hand before she got there.

'You *sod*!' She hissed.

'D'you *want* to start a riot?'

'You're forgetting what I am, Reg.' She shook her throbbing fingers out. 'I'm stealthy as a... stealthy thing. I only want to look at it.'

His face softened just a touch. She was doing that pleading little sister face; the one she used to use when she wanted him to teach her something. It hadn't changed in all the seventeen years she'd been on God's Earth, and it still made him go soft as muck.

'All right, but be quick.'

No sooner had he said it than she had the haversack in her lap and folded the flap back. The brass stock of the weapon glinted in the glow of the gaslight. The Nipper was the new favourite weapon of seamen. It had the range of the bigger rifles they used on land, but wasn't much bigger than a standard handgun. It was also one of the most powerful weapons on the market. They said you could shoot an enemy from half a nautical mile away, or a quarter if the weather was bad. Of course, you had to be a dead shot, but that was no bother for Vic. Purbright only put up with her because she was the most accurate shot in the Force, after all. Now, she'd be the most accurate shot with her very own Nipper. It was like all her Christmases had come at once, and Reggie knew it.

'It's Services grade, so make sure—'

Vic waved the warning away. 'Yeah, yeah. Super-sensitive, light pressure and all that. Got it.'

'And there's about twenty shots in the box.'

'Nice one, cheers.' She drank up and sighed. 'I'd better get going. Early day tomorrow.'

Reg leaned over and grabbed her hand.

'Here, have you settled on a bride yet?'

'Don't be daft. Who wants to settle with a killer?'

'You're not just a killer, Vic. You're a killer by royal appointment.'

'Mmm. You'd think they'd pay me more.'

They both laughed then. Vic stood up, slinging the bag with her new toy over her shoulder.

'I should make the most of this if I were you. They might not do beer at your next port.'

Reggie stood up and took her in for one final bear hug.

'Take care, sis. And make sure you put plenty of paper down on those foreign khazis.'

*

The Caeliner wasn't as big as Sapphire had imagined, even though the gondola looked the part. The figurehead of Hermes cut an interesting silhouette, even through the many ground ropes. Metal joints between the varnished wood panels shone as bright as a newly minted coin in the morning sun. The crew lining the passenger gangplanks looked prepared for a royal visit in their dress uniforms. It was just that the dirigible itself didn't look capable of carrying the weight of a thousand-person vessel. It wasn't as long as the gondola, and the propellers on the flank looked too small to function. All that, and the rudder seemed stuck out at an odd angle, like one of Aunt Gladys' teeth. Sapphire shivered as she handed her ticket over to the steward at the top of the gangplank. And not just because of the crisp December air.

'Welcome aboard, ma'am,' she said, punching the ticket with her brass snipper and handing it back.

'This balloon,' she said, holding her hat as she leant back to squint up at it. 'Is it adequate for a ship this size?'

'You've a sharp eye, ma'am. Do you often travel by liner?'

'Now and then.'

In fact, this would be her first overseas trip by air. Emmett had always preferred sea or locomotive. Not that the steward needed to know that, although she was smiling as though she saw through the lie, anyway.

'The dirigible is more than adequate for a ship this size. It's an Mk. 2 Lark, a not-so-distant cousin of the Starlings our fleet usually use.' Lord, she'd done it now. This one was a talker that liked her job and obviously didn't get asked about it much. Still, Sapphire smiled and nodded politely. 'They use a specific gas compound that gives the whole thing more lift – I can't remember its name, but you'll have noticed the thicker ground ropes?'

'Indeed. Thank you.'

She nodded at the steward and stepped aboard through the hatch. It didn't look much different to the seafaring ships she'd been on. The corridor was carpeted, and the walls were lined with intricate flocked wallpaper. Everything seemed to have a weight to it, even down to the brass portholes and the sign screwed to the wall telling her the way to the First Class check-in point. She followed it aft and joined the queue at the podium where a hubbub had got everyone whispering amongst themselves. Somewhere near the front, an indignant voice rose above the row.

'What do you mean, I'm not on this deck?'

'Sir, this is a steerage ticket.'

'It's bloody *not*.'

Sapphire craned her neck around the elderly couple in front. The young gentleman in the leather coat was waving his ticket about and wasn't having any of it. He'd picked the wrong crewman to argue with. The steward scowled back at him and narrowed his eyes over the top of his pince-nez.

'You'll need to go downstairs,' the steward told him. 'If you go back the way you came, you'll–'

'I'm with the Force, you berk!'

Sapphire bit her cheek to stifle a laugh. The steward really *did* look like a berk, and now his face was all red. It was glorious.

'Are you threatening me?'

The young man put a hand on his hip to respond, as though this whole business was making him weary.

'Listen, pal. The Force specifically requested a cabin for me on the upper deck on account of my work. They said it had all been arranged. Go and get someone who knows what they're doing, will you?'

The steward grumbled but obliged and scuttled off to find one of his colleagues. The young man put his hands in his pockets and turned with a handsome, sheepish smile to address the people he was delaying.

'Sorry about all this.'

There was a collective murmuring of quite-all-rights and not-at-alls. Sapphire stared at the man in wonder – no, he wasn't a man at all, but a young woman, she realised, taking in her embarrassed smile. She caught her eye, and the corners of the young woman's mouth turned up further. The colour rose in her face and exposed ears, and it took everything Sapphire had within her not to give a coy wave and toy with the woman even further. Had she not been saddled with Emmett, she would have liked to get to know a woman like her, she thought. What fun that would have been! The berk returned momentarily and stole back the woman's attention.

'M-my apologies, Miss Darnley. You're quite right,' he said, snatching her ticket away and presenting her with a new one, with gilded edges.

'I know I am,' she scoffed, stuffing it into her pocket. 'How about some free bevvies and I won't repeat a word?'

The berk's pince-nez looked in danger of sliding off his nose from the sweat as he hurriedly scribbled on a piece of paper. She was a wily girl, this one, and it was refreshing for Sapphire to see. So unlike the sycophants and well-mannered theatre people she was forced to deal with.

'Starboard bar,' he grumbled, and handed it over, along with a key on a tasselled fob. 'Your cabin is A37, and may your crossing be a pleasant one.'

'Aw, cheers, pal. Same to you.'

With that, she patted his face twice, with more force than Sapphire suspected she used among friends. Then she sauntered off down the corridor and turned the corner towards the passenger cabins, which were all located midship.

Sapphire wasn't entirely sure why she did it, but she stared at her ticket and silently cursed that her own cabin was listed as A88. Fortune, however, seemed to favour her that morning, as her ear picked out the voice of the old gentleman who was now at the head of the queue. He seemed to be taking umbrage to being assigned the cabin next to that 'terribly rude person'. She squeezed past the few people in front of her and waved a gloved hand to catch the berk's attention.

'Why don't I exchange cabins with this gentleman, sir? Would that be agreeable?'

*

Once checking-in was complete, the ground crew cast off the Caeliner's ropes, and the vessel ascended at speed. There was a chorus of cheers from the folk on terra firma, and from those who dared venture to the wind deck in such temperatures. Passenger trunks would arrive once they'd been matched to the passenger lists, and the ship was well into the sky, but it didn't matter to Vic. She'd only brought the old knapsack she'd come aboard with, and slung it down on the stool next to her as she perched up against the bar in the starboard lounge.

'I got told to give you that,' she said, passing the note that idiot of a steward had given her to the barman.

It didn't matter to her whether they put her in a first-class cabin or the cargo hold, but the Force had a reputation to uphold, and she might as well have tried it on for free drinks. 'Don't ask, don't get', Reg had always told her, and you had to take all you could get in this life.

'Certainly, ma'am,' the barman said, after squinting at the

paper.

He spun around and pushed up the concertina cover on the mixing deck – it was a relatively new-fangled console resembling a mechanical typewriter, which was meant to pour perfect measures once you'd punched the order in. All the gubbins that dispensed glasses and controlled the optics and barrels were cleverly hidden behind a large mural spanning the length of the lounge – it showed a kraken battling Poseidon or Neptune or some kind of sea god with a trident, and a tiny little clipper ship caught up in the middle. The mixing deck was more interesting to Vic, though, as it seemed it also acted as a cash register. Vic watched the barman punch in A37, followed by that beautiful button that read 'credit'. He handed the paper back to Vic.

'What can I get you?'

The question stumped her. She wasn't used to being offered a choice, except perhaps for beer or slightly dearer beer. To make the most of it, she was determined to have the most expensive-sounding thing she could think of.

'Dandelion and burdock?'

The barman smiled and turned to punch in the order. Vic smiled too, with the self-satisfaction of having played the system. She spun around to take in the empty lounge. It was a low-ceilinged room, as they all were on these airliners, with two large portholes on the opposite wall that flooded the place with light. A large reproductogram stood idle in the corner where a portion of the floor had been cleared for dancing. A few steam braziers were scattered between the card tables, concentrating hot air through the holes in the floor. They were doing a poor job of warming the lounge. Still, she thought she'd better get used to it. She wasn't planning on seeing much more of the ship on this crossing. At least the distant thrum of the starboard propeller was somewhat relaxing.

She knocked back the drink the barman handed her and was disgusted to taste absolutely nothing alcoholic. She grimaced, but that wasn't the most irritating thing to happen to her today. Lady Carlyle was on the same crossing as her. How was she supposed to relax and enjoy the airtime now? What if Dulcett was on board, too, and struck here and not in Somaliland as predicted? *No, don't think daft, Vic. You can't kill someone in the air without every Tom, Dick, and Harry knowing about it.* If anything, airliner passengers stuck their noses in on board affairs even more than those who travelled by sea. Funny how people enjoyed looking at the waves, but watching clouds made them nervous. She stared at the mural, as if trying to get her head around the idea. Eventually, she got lost in the painted waves, taking in every speck of foam the artist had managed to capture. She barely heard the soft voice by her shoulder.

'Pardon me, Miss Darnley – is anybody sitting here?'

Vic shrugged, oblivious, and carried on staring. That kraken – the power in those tentacles!

'Nah, love, you crack on.'

The stool to her left squeaked and the floorboards under it gave a hefty *crack* as the woman's weight settled. Vic listened to her order a Sherry Cobbler – what was *that*? She'd have to make sure to try one before landing. It sounded sickly, like a pudding or something. And then the penny dropped – how did this bint know her *name*? Unless…

It *was*, Vic realised, and her stomach lurched. Lady Carlyle was sitting next to her, sipping at a hideous orange creation in a glass that she held by the stem, with her little finger out. These poshos had a nerve. Had she followed her down here? Would she have to be *pleasant* with her?

'Do forgive my impertinence, Miss Darnley. It's my first time travelling alone, you see, and I just cannot contain myself.'

Normally a girl travelling alone was terrific news for Vic, but now it was just the opposite.

'I overheard the fracas with the steward earlier on and I wanted to express my gratitude for the marvellous job you do in London. Many's the time a fanatical has rushed me at the stage door and the Force has come to my aid. Oh, do forgive me! I'm Sapphire. Sapphire Carlyle.'

Ah! So she's dropped the Lady *bit*, thought Vic.

'Well, cheers, Sapphire. Your praise means a lot to me. My name's Vic.'

'Vic! Is that short for Victoria?'

'Yeah, but maybe don't bandy it about, eh? I don't think the Somalis are too keen on the Empire.'

Sapphire shot Vic a look – was it anger? Lawks, she didn't think the comment was an attack on *her*, did she? It was well known that her father was Indian, and there were mixed feelings among the upper set about it, even now. Or, worse, Sapphire didn't think she was an *imperialist*? Luckily, it wasn't anger at all.

'I admire your tongue, Vic. It is so refreshing to hear a young woman speak her mind. More of us should do so.'

This was getting dangerous now. Weren't opera singers meant to be ever so genteel? How was Vic supposed to keep an eye on the woman if she seemed bent on tiny acts of rebellion, as her tone seemed to indicate? She'd better keep the conversation friendly and not worry her, or put any notions in her head.

'You sing,' said Vic.

It was more of a statement than a question, but it seemed Sapphire felt obliged to answer all the same.

'I do! How perceptive of you, Vic.'

Vic nodded and reached into her inner pocket for the postcard she'd pinched from the brief for 'research'. She flashed it to Sapphire and took the opportunity to do her showing off act.

'Truth be told, I'm a bit of a fan of yours.'

That drove Sapphire's thoughts far away from rebellion. Her brown cheeks grew pink and her eyes glistened brightly in the sunlight coming in through the portholes. It seemed that when she was nervous, she was even more beautiful than the reproduced engraving she held in her hand. It shook as she stared at it.

'I-I'm flattered. Do tell me – and forgive me, for I'm ever so vain – which is your favourite opera that you've seen me in?'

Bugger. She should have seen that one coming.

'Oh, well… I don't think I could pick just one. They're all good in their own way, ain't they?'

Vic swallowed the rest of her vile drink, looking out of the corner of her eye all the while. The answer had apparently satisfied Sapphire, because now she was looking down at her lap with a silly grin on her face that most women wouldn't dare to show off in public. It made Vic want to smile, something she wasn't used to doing – and something she *mustn't* do, she realised. After all, she had a job to do and it wouldn't sit right if she got too friendly with anyone involved. She had to be professional.

'Enjoy your Sherry Wobbler,' she said, standing up. She slung one strap of her knapsack over her shoulder and nodded.

The Assassination of Lady Carlyle

'*Lady* Carlyle.'

She left the lady well and truly agog as she strode off towards her cabin.

*

You fool, Sapphire. She'd done nothing but chide herself since their conversation in the starboard lounge that afternoon, all through another Cobbler, and coming back and getting her trunk in, and changing for dinner. *Of course she would know you were Emmett's wife.* She *knew* her, had seen her perform, and it was right there on the postcard which she still had in her little snakeskin bag. She would have to return it sooner or later and hoped to see her again about the liner instead of showing up at her cabin unannounced. Travelling alone or not, it would be far too inappropriate to be seen knocking on the girl's door.

There was no trace of Vic in the first-class dining room, and on top of that, the meal was uninspired. Sapphire had hoped for something Somali, so she could prepare herself for the inevitable dining situations with the sultans and British bigwigs. Instead, what arrived was a standard beef and vegetables affair. She ate it slowly, and it felt all the more laborious because of the interminable conversations that the people sharing her table insisted upon having. Then one of the middle-aged bores had the nerve to point out they were dining with a celebrity. *Wonderful!* She had no peace at all throughout dessert until she excused herself ahead of cheese and biscuits.

It was early evening, already dark out, but still Sapphire felt the urge to go up to the wind deck. The dinner had been suffocating, and she needed to cool down and clear her head of the classist nonsense her tablemates spouted. *The liner would be over the south of France by now,* she thought. She made her way aft to the spiral iron staircase that led up to the wind deck. A heavy-set steward manned the door at the top, who wordlessly turned the handwheel as she climbed the steps. It took all his weight against the door to get it open, and an icy headwind blew in.

'It's quite safe, madam,' the steward said, smiling as she grabbed onto the handrail to steady herself. 'Just a bit cold!'

'Thank you.'

He offered a hand for her to hold as she stepped through the hatch and promptly shut the door behind her. He had been right after all – it was perfectly safe. The wind deck felt just like another corridor on the ship, albeit wider and colder. Handrails lined both sides under wide viewing spaces, which had no glass but were too high to fall over. A number of smaller portholes with glass were conveniently placed at waist height for shorter passengers, or perhaps if the deck chairs were in use. As it was, they were locked away in a container at the bow end. A handful of passengers milled about, looking over the sides in wonder. Most had had the foresight to dress appropriately, Sapphire noted, and hugged her arms around her, making sure her handbag was firmly tucked under her arm. The wind whipped her hair out of its combs as she made her way to the port side. She took hold of the handrail, and it made her stomach turn to poke her head out of the gap and look straight down. She turned her attention to the land further away. From two miles up, France looked like a rustic quilt in shades of black and grey. Here and there, lights from the villages and farms broke the landscape up. She thought of all the people living down there, and how simple and rewarding their lives must be. So often she'd played a peasant character, and so often she'd dreamed about how freeing it must be to live off the land and one's own labour for oneself, and not for the benefit of others. Perhaps this trip would be a step further towards the life she dreamed of, but had only ever played out on stage.

'Forgive the intrusion, my lady, but are you not cold?'

The voice jerked her out of her thoughts and chilled her in a way the wind didn't. She didn't even want to look at him, that crazed fanatic who often showed up at the stage door.

'How did you know I'd be here?'

'You forget, my lady – I am an admirer of yours. I follow your career closely. And this was the last liner bound for Somaliland on this side of the New Year. I couldn't miss the chance to hear you perform in a *palace*.'

It was simply no good. She had to look him in the eye – those terrifying eyes that made her feel as though she were speaking to the Devil himself. Her grip tightened on the rail as she stared Professor Dulcett down.

'Well, I do hope you enjoy the performance,' she spat.

'*There* you are, Sapph! I brought your coat!'

They both turned to see an odd young girl dressed like a docker, with her sleeves rolled, waving a leather coat at them – *Vic!* Dulcett's thin mouth was agape, to Sapphire's glee.

'You've a chaperone after all?' He asked, tiredly.

'Yes,' Sapphire lied, waving to Vic. 'Miss Darnley hasn't been in my employ long, but she's more than proved her worth already.'

She made her way over to Vic and shrugged the coat on. It was warm, though it fitted where it touched, and she took Vic's arm, which was covered in goose bumps.

'Goodnight, Professor,' she said, and gave him a reserved wave before allowing Vic to lead her back to her cabin.

If it wasn't for her, this trip would be well on its way to becoming a nightmare.

*

Vic listened to Sapphire tell her everything she knew about Dulcett when they got back to her cabin, which was right next door to Vic's – *was someone out for a laugh or something?* Sapphire had more luggage than Vic and had spread it all out across the already busy room. Upper class décor never was to Vic's taste, but she didn't mind it so much when the company was decent, even if that company was going to be the cause of a sudden and drastic career change. She might well have to give it up after this job – the stress wasn't exciting any more. It was just knackering.

'Do sit down, Vic.'

She did as she was told, in a fashion, and perched on the dressing table. Sapphire ordered a pot of tea using the messenger by her bed, which was a brass plate on the wall. You filled out a piece of paper from the little shelf, rolled it up into one of the canisters provided, and shoved it in the little round hole underneath. It then got sucked through a system of tubes to the galley where they'd get your order ready and have someone deliver it in due course. The concept was alien to Vic, and she watched in wonder as Sapphire completed the process in about ten seconds.

'I met Professor Dulcett after a performance of *Figaro* last summer,' she said, sitting on the edge of her bed. 'He came to the stage door and explained how he'd wanted to see me perform after hearing of my prowess, but his work had often prevented him from coming. I told him I was flattered, and that I hoped he liked my work. And then I signed an autograph for him, and that was that, or so I thought. There was nothing unusual in his behaviour, although he looked a bit odd. But he kept coming, you see – once a week at first, and then twice, more than even my most devoted admirers. And every time he'd – sorry, are you taking *notes*?'

Vic glanced up from her pocketbook, which she thought she'd managed to keep cleverly hidden in her lap.

'No.'

'I can see your pencil moving.'

Blast! She was getting rusty. There was no use denying it, and Sapphire wasn't an idiot. The look she was giving her said that plainly enough.

'All right, yes. Old habit – the Force, you know?'

Sapphire's face softened.

'Oh, yes. Of course.'

'D'you want to carry on, then?' Vic asked after an awkward pause.

'Sorry, yes. Well, every time Dulcett came to see me, he'd bring me little presents – it must have been quite expensive, really, being twice or sometimes three times a week and all. I felt rather embarrassed sometimes.'

'He must have been very fond of your work,' Vic noted, writing 'FOND?', underlined three times in the top corner of the page.

'I don't doubt it. But my husband didn't approve, you see. He was terribly possessive... yes, very. Flowers and pictures were all very well. He didn't mind those, but then came expensive foreign sweets, books that I liked, and things he'd been working on. Valuable things... Vic, he sent me one of his *machines*, and in his own image.'

'Dulcett sent you a Sonophone?'

'Yes. It really was an ingenious thing. It even spoke with his voice.'

Vic scratched at her temple with her pencil. Something wasn't adding up. Didn't someone have to be dead before a Sonophone could be made with their voice? She wasn't an investigator. God knew she didn't have the head for it, but this piqued her curiosity.

'Do you still have the device?'

'Sadly not. Emmett destroyed it in one of his rages before he fell ill. He stopped the Professor from coming to see me not long after that.'

'Your husband stopped him from seeing you?'

'Oh! It was nothing personal, no fisticuffs or anything like that. No, Emmett spoke to the manager of the theatre and they banned the Professor. He wasn't allowed in to watch me, and the manager personally escorted me from the stage door after every performance.'

A tired but clear knock on the door broke up the conversation. Sapphire got off the bed to answer it, and Vic felt her chest tighten as she walked past. Ever prepared, she put her hand into the leather pouch on her hip, feeling for the cold brass stock of her Nipper. Her hand took hold, and she let her finger brush up and down the trigger guard in anticipation. Had Dulcett had the brazen gall to follow them down here? Surely not, but it was always a possibility – and as an assassin, Vic was prepared for everything. Well, everything except for the will of certain posh opera singers, as today had proved.

A supervising steward in a black hussar jacket and white breeches brought in a tray. On it was a steaming china teapot and two matching cups upturned on saucers. Vic took her hand out of the pouch, slumping with a bit of relief, before rubbing her hands together.

'Lovely pot of char, ta.'

The steward scowled and looked her up and down. *Bloody cheek! It wouldn't hurt her to smile,* Vic thought, seeing as they'd obviously seen fit to let supervisors deal with the better of the first-class set. What a pack of bustle-kissers. The steward set the tray down on the bedside table. She glared at Sapphire as she told her, begrudgingly, that she needed only put the tray outside for a refill and that she wished her a good night. Shame the face didn't match what came out of her mouth.

The china did, though, Vic noted, as she turned her attention to the intricate flower patterns. It wasn't something she was used to, and the cups looked like they might break if she held one too hard. She heard the door shut behind the steward, but a muted burst of laughter made her look up.

'Oh, Vic!' Sapphire managed between chuckles. 'That was priceless!'

'What?'

'Nobody ever addresses stewards when they come to the room! I do believe you've made history, my dear!'

'Made history, eh?' Vic liked the sound of that, and smirked. 'But why doesn't anyone talk to–'

She didn't get to finish as the ship tilted violently to the starboard side and she was thrown off the dressing table. She fell forward with a lurch and put her hands out to steady herself against the cabin wall. Sapphire had managed to save the teapot, but everything else in the cabin that wasn't fixed down was thrown to one side.

'What was that?'

Sapphire's voice was quiet, something Vic would never expect of an opera singer. That was the sound of terror, but she was happy to quell her fears.

'Bit of turbulence,' Vic said, righting herself as the tilt of the ship levelled back out. 'It's fairly normal, but never that... intense. Wind must be strong.' *Like a bad day in Reg's undercrackers*, she added silently. 'Come on, let's have some—'

Another sickening lurch back to starboard had her on the floor.

'Oh, come off it!' She hollered to nobody in particular.

She scrambled to her feet and held onto the fixtures as she made her way to the door.

'Are you all right, Vic?' Sapphire shouted from underneath a pile of clothes and books.

The teapot had also disappeared.

'Wait there,' Vic told her, satisfied she was unharmed.

She opened the door, which fell back with a bang.

Outside in the corridor, it was like some avant-garde painting. Everything was at a slant, so much so that Vic had to look up to the cabins on the opposite side. Further down the corridor, a middle-aged woman was in a heap on the floor, having apparently come out of her door at the wrong moment. The sour-faced steward who'd brought the tea was helping her up. A few brave passengers stood at their doors, clinging onto handrails and light fixtures as they looked up and down with puzzled looks but didn't dare speak.

'Oi, mate, what's going on?' Vic asked the man two doors down.

He shrugged before a piercing howl echoed through the corridor and made them both wince. A gruff voice followed through the communication grill on the aft wall.

'All Eagle crew report to the wind deck immediately.'

Vic's stomach turned over. She knew from what Reg had told her that there were animal names that people in the Services used in order not to give away information; a bit like codenames for robberies in the Regent Street Shops. She'd been called Miss Brown once or twice when she'd tried to lift a few years ago. Going by the name, the Eagle crew had to work topside, which could only mean that something was wrong with the ship. Sapphire bent forward on the bed as she held her hands over her ears.

'What can we do, Vic?' She cried.

'I'm going to take a look.'

'*You?*' Her head snapped up. 'What can you do?'

'I don't know,' Vic lied, 'but stay here. Don't move unless they give the order to evacuate.'

In fact, there were a lot of things she could do. She climbed out of the cabin, shutting the door on Sapphire. She walked along the skirting board, nimble as a ropewalker in a circus, to her own cabin next door, where she shrugged on her knapsack. Climbing wouldn't be an issue – she'd done plenty of it in her time, scaling the tallest of buildings for a long-range target and running across roofs and spires when she needed to make a quick exit. And she was strong, and could follow orders when she needed to. There had to be something useful she could do.

The way to the wind deck was awkward at a slant, but she managed better than some of the staff she saw going about the ship, telling people to stay calm and keep to their cabins. It was hard to hear them over that terrible din of a siren. She worked her way up to the next deck, and then aft to the staircase where the Eagle crew, some who'd been off-duty, were scrambling and sodding about with wind-suits and ropes. She climbed over light fixtures towards one of the more competent members of the crew, who'd already rigged herself up. She had multiple tool belts criss-crossing her back and was about to head up – or rather, over the staircase.

'Who's in charge here, love?'

'Sir, passengers are not permitted up to the wind deck at the moment,' the woman said, adjusting her goggles. 'Please go back to your cabin.'

'Nah, look – I'm with the Force,' said Vic, pulling her badge out of her pocket. 'Police, Royal Division. Isn't there something I can do?'

The woman squinted at the badge and nodded.

'My apologies, Miss Darnley. Here.' She unhooked a set of goggles from the collection tangled on the wall, and gave them to her. 'How's your balance?'

'Good enough,' said Vic, adjusting the leather strap at the back of her head.

'All right. We've no more harnesses, but tie this around you.'

Vic did as she was told, though she knew she wouldn't need it, and tied the thick rope around her waist, making sure the metal hook at the end was secure on the lashing point. Then they climbed over the steps up to the hatch to the wind deck, where the head engineer was waiting.

'She's police!' The woman shouted over the wind, in answer to her superior's quizzical stare.

'Fine!' He yelled. 'The seal's gone on the propeller shaft, starboard flank. Stopped working. We've not lost altitude, thank God, but the port side can't handle it on its own for much longer. Jones and Adedayo already assessed the damage. We need someone to hook up the lift on the casing for you, Simmons.'

'I can do it,' Vic volunteered, already unhooking herself from Simmons.

She knew she'd be quicker than any of the crew, unencumbered by any of that additional safety gear.

'It's a rough job,' said Simmons.

'I said I can do it.'

Nobody dared to argue with her. Two wind-suited crewmen wheeled a wire cage and what seemed to be mounds of rope and fixings towards them. Vic was putting the lift together in her mind. Those four hooks with the chains hooked over the metal frame (*casing, Vic*), that bit was the puller-upper-and-downer – she didn't know the technical terms, but she could see what was what. She attached the four hooks to her belt, and swapped her knapsack for two thick coils of rope. It all weighed her down, but she could still move, just about, as she made for the ratlines leading up to the propeller. She didn't listen to the crew who seemed to be having a collective breakdown, crying about safety lines and lunacy and death. She could barely hear them for the wind anyway. The chain ladder up to the ratlines was normal enough, and went straight up. She grabbed hold of it from inside, and climbed out of the viewing gap to swing into position, facing the wind deck. She ascended quickly, and had she looked back at the crew she would have seen them gasp and cover their eyes. Now came the tricky bit. The balloon, like the gondola, was at a slant, and the ratlines that would have gone straight up were instead above her head. She grasped onto the lines directly above her and used all her strength to swing her feet up like a monkey. Now she was hanging upside down, and stared straight across at clouds in the night sky, with only the light of the moon to show her where to move next.

The climb up – that was upside down and forward – was harder than she'd anticipated. Not only did she have to use all her strength to keep from falling, she also had to face the wind and it was still a December night. Her fingers were numb, and her face stung as if an army of wasps was attacking her from all angles. All that, and the Nipper was still at her hip. Any jerky movement could open the pouch and she'd have to kiss it goodbye. That would never do, she'd have to find a more traditional, more boring means of doing Dulcett in.

Vic Darnley, you utter foozler! He was somewhere on the ship, and she'd left Sapphire in her cabin *alone*. The realisation made her feel sick. The ratlines in front of her whirled about in her vision like she'd had too much beer. She put a hand to her forehead to try to stop the sensation until she remembered the pull of gravity and clung back on. She had to get this done fast. Against anyone's better judgement, she moved up the lines two rungs at a time. Her heart jumped up to her throat as one of her feet slipped off, and the weight of the lift line wanted to bring her back down to earth.

'Get it together, Vic,' she muttered.

The propeller was another twenty feet away, and she could already see where the seal had come away from the shaft – or rather, had been blown off. The metal was scorched, and the casing around the propeller had bowed from the heat. Vic sniffed as she climbed towards it – yes, it was unmistakable. The greasy stink of the oil-paste adhesive, mixed in with sulphur – someone had tried to blow the propeller clean off with a sticking-bomb. They were mainly used in demolition or the Services, or sometimes by the Force, being lightweight and easy to handle. Either way, it was a wonder the heat hadn't burst the balloon.

Hot air was shooting out into the night from one half of the shaft, turning to steam where it met the cold. The other half wobbled helplessly, supported by a couple of iron rods that somehow didn't look capable of supporting the propeller itself. Vic clambered up to it and manoeuvred to sit astride the bowed casing. The hot air burned her face as she took off two hooks and attached them to the strut, pulling hard to make sure they wouldn't go anywhere. The chains clanged as she slid to the end. She had to hold on to the corner strut as she attached the other two. Finally, the chains fell and made a taught cross on the underside of the casing. It was easy then – a bit more shimmying and threading ropes through lashing points, and her part was nearly done. She loosely tied the ends of the ropes together, and put the knot under her arm for the climb down, which she managed a lot more quickly without the extra weight of the metal. Back on the wind deck, the lift was ready to go, and Vic dumped the ropes in Simmon's arms as soon as she landed.

'That'll have to do you, love,' she said, sweating in spite of the vicious wind. 'I've got something I need to see to.'

'Very well, Miss Darnley – and thank you!'

Vic sped back down the stairs two at a time, even at an angle, and pulled her goggles down. It was only as they bounced against her collarbone that she remembered they weren't hers – never mind, returning them could wait. She tore through the passages back to Sapphire's cabin quicker than a steward summoned by the bell. The door was open, cracking against the wood panelling, and all was as she'd left it. Sapphire, however, was gone.

'Bloody poshos, do as they please!' muttered Vic.

She turned on her heel and looked up and down the corridor. Not a soul was around, worse luck. Should she try the privies? That would be the obvious place to look – the incident would have set more than a few stomachs turning, no doubt. She made her way forward towards the bow where the privies were located, but skidded to a halt where the passage was blocked by a red rope. The berk with the pince-nez was there, standing to attention like a sentry, and Vic scowled.

'You again?'

'Indeed,' he said, as though bored by the whole situation. 'Did your ears fail you? First-class passengers must muster in the dining room, all other passengers in the hold. Seems you've a choice, *miss*,' he spat.

'Well, I didn't hear any announcement, pal. I was too busy saving your ruddy ship! Bit of respect wouldn't hurt for saving your life.'

Vic smirked as she left him, mouth quivering with the lack of something to say. She sprinted down to the first-class dining room, which was at a slant like everything else. The tables and chairs had all crashed down to the starboard side where the portholes were, and had been cordoned off with more red ropes. Not that they were readily visible, because every first-class passenger, all two hundred or so, were packed in and standing around idle. Reason suggested that there should have been a great panicked hubbub, but instead there was music. An ethereal voice filled the room and the souls of all who heard it. It was a foreign language that Vic didn't understand, but a sense of calm and awe washed over her all at once, to the point that she felt tears threatening to surface. That may well have been because she knew now she hadn't ruined her mission, and Sapphire was safe. She shouldered her way through the crowd toward her, trying hard to fight back the tears that had come forward anyway – she hadn't cried in years, and definitely wasn't about to in front of an audience. Anyway, it was bound to be because of her tiring feat and not because of something as useless as relief.

Sapphire's song came to a climactic end, and was met with a round of polite, calculated applause. It didn't seem emphatic enough, so Vic whistled and swung her goggles above her head. That got Sapphire's attention. After she'd asked a steward to set up a reproductogram, she charged toward Vic and grabbed her hand. She led her away from the ogling sycophants and out into the entrance vestibule where the menus were kept.

'You ain't half got a pair of lungs on you, Sapphire,' said Vic, sniffing hard.

Any other time Sapphire would have melted at the praise, but instead she only shoved her, and hard.

'Where did you *go*? You were gone an age!'

'Yeah, I ended up doing the crew's work for them. But at least the liner's safe,' she said, gesturing to the chandelier in the dining room.

It was creeping towards a straight hang rather than a skew one as the ship slowly righted itself.

'But what of *me*? The Professor came to me again, Vic! It was only the muster order that got rid of him.'

Vic nodded, and her heart pounded in her ears as she realised the implication. She wanted to tell Sapphire how she'd raced to find her the minute she knew she was in danger, but there were more serious matters to attend to.

'Where is he now?'

'I'm not sure. He ran towards the dining room with the other passengers, but when I turned to look for him, he'd disappeared.'

A strong crosswind wobbled the ship, and the party inside the dining room started a loud panic. Vic stared at Sapphire, but saw only the propeller shaft in her mind's eye. She would have smelled the sticking-bomb too, if her mind had had a nose equivalent.

'I think I know where he might be,' Vic said, putting her goggles back on. 'Go and wait in there!'

And she left Sapphire alone. Again.

*

No more. Sapphire had an unfathomable fondness for Vic, but she wasn't about to listen to her again. Not after she'd left her at the mercy of that obsessive Professor. What would happen if Vic's suspicion was unfounded, and he came back? No, she'd feel much safer with her – she was a member of the Force, after all.

She caught a glimpse of Vic's coat as she turned into the corridor that led aft. Sapphire ran after her, which was easier said than done in her evening dress. At least the ship was nearly level again. She didn't dare shout out to anger or distract Vic, but was a good many paces behind her. On more than one occasion, she thought she'd lost her. Golly, but the girl could move!

The chase led her to the wind deck, where two engineers were reeling the last of the ropes back onto a heavy spool. They took no notice of her, or indeed Vic, who seemed about ready to climb out of the viewing space; her feet were on the handrail and an arm was crooked around one of the roof supports.

'No!'

To Sapphire, it seemed it had just slipped out – but it was loud, even audible over the blast of the headwind. Vic's head snapped around, and she looked furious and ruddy-faced. Sapphire, on the other hand, felt the cold weight of guilt settle on her.

'What are you doing?' demanded Vic as she hopped down from her terrifying position. She marched over to Sapphire. 'Didn't I tell you to stay below?'

'I couldn't let you go, not again.' *Silly girl*, she thought, as her voice cracked. 'I need you, Vic. You make me feel so very safe, and I couldn't bear being alone with all those people. What if the Professor...?'

Vic's shoulders slumped, and against everything her head was telling her, she held her arms out to the crying girl. Sapphire fell into them, burying her head in Vic's shirt, and holding fast to her waist lest she should collapse from the different emotions that were battling for precedence. Joy promised to appear as she felt Vic's fingers brush gently over her hair and felt her warm breath on her forehead.

'It's all right, Sapph,' she said, though it really wasn't.

Dulcett hadn't yet ventured up on deck to try and blow the other propeller. Of course he wouldn't, if the engineering team were still hanging about. No, he'd wait until he was able to throw a sticking-bomb, unencumbered by staff or others who might see him. Meanwhile, there was an entire ship he could hide away in, and different areas to attack.

'Come on,' Vic said. She put an arm around Sapphire and turned her back towards the stairwell. 'Let's get a drink and go back to the cabin, eh? I won't leave you alone again.'

'Now that does rather complicate things, doesn't it?'

Vic felt Sapphire grow tense at the sound of that terrible voice behind them. From out of the gloom towards the far end of the wind deck stepped Dulcett, who had apparently waited for the last few crewmen to disappear. Sure enough, he held a sticking-bomb in his hand, as Vic had expected, but something was wrong. His face was whiter than the stars, even in the dim light of the wind deck. He was shaking from top to toe. *Don't panic*, she thought, *nothing's changed. You've still got to kill the man, even if it is in front of her.*

'Listen to me. Don't do anything rash, Sapph,' whispered Vic, tightening her grip around her.

She couldn't go for her Nipper, not with his eyes on them both. Suppose he should throw the bomb right at them?

'I wanted to make it look like an accident!' Dulcett said, his eyes wide. 'I wanted to give you some dignity.'

Vic stiffened and tried her hardest to keep her voice level.

'You meant to *kill* her, man. Where's the dignity in that?'

Sapphire gasped and stared at her. Though she couldn't read her face, if she'd had the gift she would have known that Vic's head was screaming a stronger word at the man than she'd ever come across.

'Professor...' she paused and looked at him as he inched ever closer. 'You want to kill me?'

'You don't understand, your ladyship!' He raised the sticking-bomb above his head as he started to weep. 'How could you ever understand?'

'Oh! Don't give us all that, Dulcett,' snarled Vic, as she watched the pathetic man bury his face into his empty hand. *Perhaps he ought to be on the stage, too, what with all this drama.* 'What's this – changed your tune, have you? You don't want her voice box for your machine after all?'

She'd said something wrong. She must have done. The Professor began to howl like one of the men she'd seen in Bedlam many years ago. It chilled her as much now as it had then, and she took the moment his head was held back to grasp for her Nipper.

'Silly girls and their silly notions! Though I'd be a liar if I said that the thought hadn't crossed my mind – yes, you'd get rather a lot of interest in a Sonophone in your ladyship's likeness, no doubt. Though it's just as easily done if the subject co-operates. My team and I have been developing a new method of sound reproduction, you see – you needn't use the vocal chords at all, just record every phonetic sound onto the plates and then you'll have–'

'All right, mate, I've got it,' Vic said. She was starting to lose interest in the ins and outs of it all. This new technology would explain his ghastly gift to Sapphire, anyway, and she'd make sure to brief Purbright on it once she got back to London. 'But get to the point – why would you murder this poor girl?'

Sapphire's eyes began to well at the very thought.

'Don't you see? It's the only way we could ever be together. Better the demise of Lady Carlyle was reported as one of many lives lost in a tragic airship malfunction than a filthy backstreet murder.'

'Together? Us? You're no better than Emmett!' Sapphire shrugged Vic's hand off her shoulder and began to inch towards the Professor. 'Honestly, I've never had the chance to decide anything in my entire life. Forever ruled by men who think themselves better than everyone else – what makes you the exception?'

'Sapphire, watch it,' Vic said, noting Dulcett's frantic breathing.

Should she strike now? But there wasn't a clear shot, not with Sapphire in front.

'I've dedicated my life to naught but sound,' he said. 'How fitting it should end with a soprano's scream!'

He drew his arm back and launched the sticking-bomb at them.

'DOWN!' Vic cried.

Wrenching the crewman's goggles from around her neck, she leapt over Sapphire and thrust them forward. They met the bomb like a bat meeting a ball. The bomb stuck fast, and she swung the goggles not just once, but twice, before launching the thing out of the nearest viewing space and far into the frosty night air. It flew magnificently, like a misshapen bird, before falling towards the ground. Nobody on the ship saw the explosion, but there was a slight bump from underneath the port side that barely rocked the vessel.

'You fool,' hissed Dulcett, glaring at Vic. He felt inside his coat for another bomb. 'You've failed!'

'No, I haven't.'

She grinned and took aim. The Nipper was every bit as good as she dreamed it would be.

The Assassination of Lady Carlyle

*

'FIELD REPORT AT HER MAJESTY'S REQUEST

Submitted by Agent Victoria Darnley on this day, 22nd December 1862, British Embassy, Somaliland

Re: Death of Lady Sapphire Carlyle

Following the assignment brief as given to myself by GOV. PHILEAS PURBRIGHT a week ago target PROFESSOR ARTHUR DULCETT was exterminated by means of GUNSHOT WOUND TO HEAD on the night of 19th December. Cadaver was observed by STEWARDS PATEL and FINCHLEY and moved to Caeliner cargo hold by the ship's medical team. Cadaver was received on landing in Somaliland by Force representatives FARAH and AHMED on 21st December. The exterminated's intended subject LADY SAPPHIRE CARLYLE was treated by DOCTOR MILLICENT BURROWS on the night of 19th December for shock and also bronchial complaint as a result of wind/cold exposure. I did not leave the subject's cabin that night or the next.

'Further to assignment brief, I carried out a duty to LADY SAPPHIRE CARLYLE and gave verbal confirmation that I would accompany her to the embassy where she would be subjected to interview by REPRESENTATIVES FARAH and AHMED before her work engagement, as disclosed to me in cabin on the night of 19th December. En route to the embassy on the date of 21st December, LADY SAPPHIRE CARLYLE was exterminated by means of ELEPHANT CHARGE. Efforts were made by myself to resuscitate at scene, but were unsuccessful. Cadaver was witnessed by VILLAGER ARI and awaits transport to England in Caeliner cargo hold. Here ends report.'

Reg scowled.

'It's a bit clinical, isn't it?' he said, trying not to get caught up on longer words he didn't understand.

It was hard enough to read in the light from the coloured glass lamps hanging in the place anyway, and the crossing had completely worn him out. He'd much rather have slept the time away, or seen the pyramids, but it wasn't often he and his sister found themselves in the same foreign continent.

'I know, it's vile. But the Force insists on it for clarity.'

Vic took the paper back and folded it before putting it in the slit in her coat that she'd laid out next to her. It was easier said than done when you were sitting on the floor and someone from the next table was sitting right up your back. She picked up the stoneware cup in front of her and squinted at the steaming red contents.

'What did you say this was?'

'It's called *Karkade*.' Sapphire grinned. 'It's hibiscus, try it.'

'And corpses trampled by elephants are quiet. Try it.'

'How can I? You've given me a stonker of a Christmas present, Vic.'

Vic scoffed. 'What, a drink in some unfurnished hole?'

'I was thinking more about my freedom,' Sapphire laughed. 'Thank you.'

She leant across the low table and curled her fingers around Vic's neck before pulling her nearer to kiss her saviour. Vic's cheeks coloured quickly. She wasn't used to receiving affection, and especially not in front of her brother. He made like a gentleman and looked away towards the door and the marketplace beyond, keeping his glee to himself.

'Well, then,' said Vic, 'I'd like to propose a toast – to the death of Lady Carlyle.'

And it was bottoms up all around.

The Clockwork Girl
by N. J. McKay

Melmoor was not the picturesque city it used to be. The white stone buildings that once gleamed in the sunlight were now covered in dirt and grime. They were stained by soot from past bombs and fires. Many were abandoned. Their owners packed up what remained and left the city for a safer existence far away from the war. Looting became a hobby for those that stayed behind as supplies stalled or stopped all together. One now had to shuffle over broken glass, scour empty shelves, or dig through collapsed buildings to find anything useful these days.

Yet the citizens of Melmoor persisted. It was their stubbornness, or their faith in the Grand Masters, that kept them from running to the hills. The Grand Masters were master craftsman from all disciplines: steam, clockwork, wood, blacksmithing and engineering. They worked together, creating extra safeguards, artillery, and inventions to protect the people of the great country of Olynana. Their tower stood like a beacon of hope in the middle of the city. Its large white stone walls towered over every other building. It glistened in the light, completely untouched by the destruction of war that plagued the rest of the city.

It reminded Sadie McLachlan of an oppressive monument, built to keep the citizens of Melmoor aware of their genius, while under their control. She hated the Tower. No matter where she went, she could see some spire or window through the narrow and crooked alleyways. It felt like something or someone was always watching.

The thought made the teenager shiver as she wrapped the thin wool coat tighter around her body. The coat felt looser this spring. She must have lost more weight over the winter than she thought. It wasn't a surprise. Everyone in Melmoor felt the pinch. Almost every supply route coming in either by road, rail, or boat had slowed to a crawl. Food was becoming scarce. The desperate stole from bakeries and stores, only for the Night Watch to catch them a few minutes later.

Dressed in black, the Grand Masters helped organise the Night Watch to aid the city during the war. They were originally meant to patrol the streets at night, watch the skies for enemy bomber planes or blimps, and search and confiscate whatever sneaky new inventions the Masters from the enemy country of Ashrath created to spy on Melmoor with.

However, times have changed. The Night Watch soon evolved into an intelligence agency. They were now trained to catch spies, traitors and anyone else they suspected as agents of Ashrath. They grew in numbers so quickly that even the local police force could no longer stand in their way. Many changed sides and soon there were no other police left but the Night Watch. They were everywhere, day and night, taking the curfew the Grand Masters put in place seriously. The Night Watch interrogated anyone wandering outside after hours and were unafraid to use violence and force to get answers. Hearing yells and screams on the streets at night was now a common occurrence, and many learned to turn a deaf ear to the pleas for mercy. Anyone caught on the streets was beaten, taken to jail, or worse, never heard from again. Sadie suspected many fled the city because of the growth and abuse of the Night Watch rather than from the war itself.

Sadie scowled at a nearby Night Watchman as he strode past. His back was straight, his chin was up, and he was walking with an air of overconfidence and superiority. A young kid sold newspapers from on top of a wooden crate on a nearby corner.

He yelled out the headlines of the day to the crowds of people who scampered past. Few stopped these days. Sadie remembered how people used to linger and socialise with each other as they made their way home for the evening. With the curfew at eight, everyone rushed to the safety of their homes.

The headlines the boy shouted were nothing new to Sadie.

'President Turner of Olynana refuses Ashrath's demands! Peace Treaty still in limbo! Turner refuses to back down from Ashrath's bullying, declaring peace will prevail!'

The ceasefire had lasted six months. Six months with no confirmation that the war would end. Yet, six months of not having any bombs, soldiers, or active battles happening in the city either. While others hoped and trusted their President and the Grand Masters with their safety, Sadie feared this was only the calm before the storm. By the state of things, she doubted Melmoor could withstand another attack if the peace treaty fell through.

Sadie's light brown eyes turned to the sky, eyeing the colourful pinks, reds, and violets as the sun set. The clock on the Tower told her it was twenty minutes to eight. It didn't give her a lot of time to search through the piles of debris and rubble from abandoned lots before the curfew bell rung.

She hated being forced to stoop to this life of petty crime, but the clockwork shop she operated needed parts. Every little bit helped. Not only had the supply chain slowed the incoming of food but also the much-needed raw materials that any craftsman required for their livelihood. Materials such as metals, gears, springs, screws, and all those small parts she needed to keep her shop afloat.

Her grandfather started McLachlan Clockworks sixty years

ago. Back when he was only eighteen and fresh out of the Tower. He ran that shop until his dying day, pouring all his blood, sweat and tears into making his business a success. It was a success that came and was now on the verge of disappearing. It was the only thing Sadie had left to remember her grandfather and mother by. She grew up in that shop. Watched them create amazing and beautiful possessions; singing mechanical birds, miniature flying aeroplanes, and ornate music boxes with tiny mechanical ballerinas that danced to the music. She promised them both at their graves that she'd do whatever it took to keep the shop open in their memory.

Sadie never broke a promise.

Sticking close to the shadows, to avoid as many Night Watchmen as possible, Sadie reached her destination on the corner of Ivy Lane and Mill Street. There, an old red brick, two story factory building stood. It was once a textile factory that closed its doors because of the interruption of the cotton and silk trade by the war. The factory did as much as they could to stay open, but like with every other major industry in the city, most of their raw materials came through Ashrath, which stopped once the war began.

Sadie surveyed the old building, looking for a way inside. A chain and lock barred her from using the front door. The shattered and broken glass windows seemed to be her only way in, but were too high for her to reach alone. Exploring the western side, Sadie spotted a pile of old crates and wooden boards stacked up against the wall, giving her a way into one of those open windows.

Climbing the crates and heaving herself into the building, Sadie quickly went to work. She scoured all the old steam-powered machines on the first floor, prying up as many cogs and gears as she could and placing them in her bag. Unfortunately, many of the machines here used parts that were far too large for her needs. Still, beggars can't be choosers. She heard on the streets that local Blacksmiths were paying decent coin for scrap metal they could smelt down and repurpose.

The sky darkened outside the broken windows. She could hear the faint ticking of the large tower clock. Her bag, now weighed down with metal parts, would slow her down, and she dared not risk pushing her luck as the curfew approached. Sadie rushed back to the old, rickety metal staircase, making a mental note to search the second floor on her next available evening, when a stray of random light glimmered off an object out of the corner of her eye.

A massive pile of debris from the caved in roof occupied the space off to her right. That wasn't what caught her attention. Something thin and long rose out of the pile like a gravestone. Edging herself closer, Sadie glanced up to see a large hole in the second floor above it, and above that a sizeable hole in the roof. At least she was correct in assuming part of the ceiling caved in on itself.

Could it be a bomb? One from the last air raid from six months ago? That still didn't explain the object that stood out from the pile. Now closer, Sadie could tell it wasn't metal, but a porcelain white arm.

Sadie felt her heart pound in her chest, and her breathing quickened. The arm seemed frozen, stiff and reaching out for some unseen aide to pull it out of its current situation. Now, she's seen dead bodies before. With all the bombing and skirmishes in the streets, death became a common part of life. Yet this arm didn't appear normal.

Taking a deep breath to steady her nerves, Sadie stepped towards the pile and reached out to touch the arm. It was cold and hard as a rock. Whatever fear that was building up inside of her subsided as curiosity took over. She gripped the arm tightly and pulled. There was no way to prepare for what happened next. The arm dislodged from the rubble, but it was only an arm. At the break there was no muscle, blood, or bone. Instead, Sadie stared down at a bunch of wires, tubes, cogs and deformed metal frame.

'What the...' Sadie whispered, her voice echoing in the large space. 'A mannequin? No... that's not it...' Her eyes grew wide and bright as a theory came to mind. 'An automaton!'

Sadie's voice rang out around her as she gaped at the wonder she now held in her hands. She remembered her grandfather and mother built little miniature ones for music boxes and toys, but they never worked on one that was life-sized before. The outer coating looked like porcelain, the same as a child's doll. Yet, as Sadie rapped it with her knuckles, she realised it was much stronger. It had to be to take a fall like that and not shatter. The curious new material had Sadie puzzled. She wondered what this automaton was really made of.

'Let's see if I can find the rest of you,' Sadie added, setting the arm down before diving into the pile.

A few minutes later she discovered a left leg, a torso with the other arm and leg still attached, and at long last, the head.

Laying the body parts out, Sadie stepped back and stared at what she found. The automaton wasn't like anything she'd seen before. Its porcelain shell coating gave it a doll-like appearance, which unsettled her. The face was incredibly lifelike, with tangled long strawberry blonde hair. A fragmented web-like crack covered most of the left eye and temple. If it wasn't in pieces, Sadie would have mistaken it for an actual human.

'Somebody put a lot of care and attention into you...' Sadie muttered as she knelt down by the head.

If that was the case, how did such a beautifully sculpted and crafted automaton end up here, broken? Sadie frowned. As a maker herself, she couldn't imagine having one of her own pieces damaged and discarded in such a horrific and disrespectful way. It made her sad.

'It's blasphemy if you ask me,' Sadie said, talking to the automaton. 'You're something to marvel at, respect, awe, even admire in a museum or up on stage. It's a shame, really, seeing someone's work torn up like this.'

Sadie sighed. She could feel her chest constrict and felt the oncoming tears well up in her eyes. Her heart seemed to break over this beautiful object. However, before she could think of what to do, she heard the first strike of the clock as it hit eight.

'Crap!' Sadie jumped to her feet.

She took two steps towards the stairs and stopped. She peered back at her discovery. The automaton was laid out like a human being in their last dying moments, silently asking for help. There was no way Sadie could leave her in that condition, alone.

With a heavy sigh, and shaking hands, she stuffed the arm, leg, and head into her bag while lifting the torso over her shoulder. She hurried out of the building; the last rays of the sun faded quickly behind the buildings. The street lights were already lit as Sadie half carried, half dragged the automaton across side streets and back alleys to avoid the Night Watchmen on patrol.

It took longer than normal to get back home, but the moment Sadie burst through the back door and laid the remains of the automaton on the workbench, she couldn't help but laugh at her luck.

'Well, looks like you won't be broken for long. Welcome to your new home.'

*

It took Sadie days to put the automaton girl back together. If she could close shop and work non-stop, she could have done it in half the time, but commissions came first, even if it was just fixing a broken pocket watch. Money was money, and very little came through the shop these days. Still, with every spare second Sadie had, she worked on the automaton.

She started calling it Cali and spoke to her as if she could hear and understand her. She spoke like that with many of her inventions or whatever she was working on. It was a habit she shared with her grandfather that made the shop less lonely.

It was the third day since bringing the doll back to the shop that Sadie finally found the maker's mark on the casing that surrounded the automaton's core. The mark every mechanic, craftsman, inventor and technician used to signify and claim their work. Her grandfather used to use a large roman case "M" with a small "c" hanging from the middle. Sadie had taken the "Mc" design from her grandfather but changed it to a smaller case "mc" to show a younger generation.

This mark, like with the rest of the automaton, was unusual. The more she tinkered with it, the more questions she had. The maker's mark had a flourish style to it, all encased within a circle with what looked like mathematical or rune like symbols instead of letters. Sadie knew every maker's and craftsman's mark in the city, and this symbol didn't line up with any of them. She had to assume that maybe it belonged to a new Maker in the Tower. Or, and this thought worried her, someone created Cali outside of Melmoor... possibly outside of Olynana.

'Unique design, disrespectfully broken and discarded, and now you contain a mark that doesn't belong here,' Sadie sighed. Her shoulders sagged as she rolled her neck to work out a kink. 'You're a curious one, aren't you, Cali? You know, my mother always said every girl has her mystery... but this is downright bizarre.'

A knock on the back door startled Sadie. It was more of a heavy pounding than a pleasant knocking. Sadie felt the stool she was leaning back on wiggle before she fell off and landed on the stone floor, taking half of her toolbox with her.

'Ouch,' Sadie seethed as the pounding continued, now more demanding than the first time.

She glanced over at the window, noticing how dark it was outside before moving her eyes to the old coo-coo-clock hanging above the entrance to the front end of the workshop. It was almost midnight and far too late for customers, or even friends, to visit.

'Night Watch! Open Up!' Came the deep voice outside the door.

'Coming!' Sadie shouted. 'What the blazing hell are they doing here?' She added in a softer, muttering tone.

Sadie glanced around the room, realising that Cali stood out like a sore thumb if they were doing an inspection or raid. She quickly grabbed an old tarp and covered Cali and the workbench before running to the back door. She reached for the knob and took three deep breaths to settle the growing amount of anxiety that now flooded her veins.

'What is the meaning of this? It's almost midnight!' Sadie said the moment she opened the door.

The trick was to sound confident and intimidating all at once by trying to shock or dismantle the other's guard. Her mother was a pro at this. However, staring up at the six foot Night Watchman, Sadie's confidence plummeted and her voice that started out strong fizzled out.

'Inspection,'

The Watchman pushed Sadie aside and marched right into the workshop, followed by his partner who was a skinny man, not much taller than her. 'There's been a report of enemy devices spying around the Tower.'

'Enemy devices?' Sadie questioned.

She heard nothing about that from the kid with the paper.

'Spying machines that hover and fly in the air without making a sound.'

'No sound? That's hard to believe,' Sadie said, trying once more to stand her ground and sound confident. She followed the large Watchman around, yanking things out of his hand and putting them back in its place. 'If you're looking for enemy inventions, look closer around the Tower. There's nothing here worth spying on.'

'We shot one down the other week, though we've yet to find the remains.'

'You mean debris,' Sadie said with a roll of her eyes. Remains makes it sounds like there's a body... 'Hey, careful over there!'

Sadie rushed to cut the large man off as he lifted the corner of the cloth over Cali and her workbench.

'What'cha got under there, girl?'

'A custom order! It's private and I'm supposed to keep it secret until it's ready.'

'A custom order?' The Watchman gave a hearty laugh and elbowed his partner to do the same. 'Who in Melmoor has enough cash to do a custom order? Not to mention McLachlan Clockworks isn't what it used to be.'

Sadie felt her face go red, but she was smart enough to bite her tongue.

'Aw well… at least you're not one of those cowards running out of town as of late.' The Watchman backed away from the tarp and moved back towards the door. 'But keep your eyes open for any suspicious contraptions and tech that may stumble its way in here for you to fix.'

'Yeah, sure…' Sadie said, her voice a low grumble.

'Also, let us know if you find anything unusual on the streets,' the second Watchman added. 'The enemy's spying device went down somewhere around Mill Street and Ivy Lane.'

Sadie felt her heart beat extra hard. Her face paled, and she felt sweat drip down her forehead.

'What did you say? Mill and Ivy?'

'Yes, well around there… like Officer Dalton said, we've been looking for the past week for the debris to analyse. If Ashrath is defying the ceasefire, the war would start up again.'

'Yes… will do…' Sadie said, though her voice sounded small and far away.

The moment the two Watchmen exited her workshop, she closed and bolted the door shut. She walked back into the workshop and pulled the tarp off of Cali. Were they looking for her? A spy for Ashrath? Sadie shook her head and paced around the workshop, which wasn't that large.

'Why are you getting so antsy, Sadie? It's just a clockwork doll! An automaton from some circus,' Sadie said.

She wrung her hands together, her eyes never leaving the soft, emotionless face of the automaton. She had Cali almost completed by now. Her head and limbs were all attached, and most of what Sadie's been working on now was replacing old or broken internal parts beneath the outer porcelain shell.

Sadie took a deep breath, telling herself over and over that the Night Watchmen were mistaken; that Cali was harmless and not a threat or danger to the safety of Melmoor. With a steady hand, Sadie returned to work within the torso, prying off a metal plate revealing the core.

A bright streak of red light filled the workshop. She expected to find a wind-up mechanism, the same technology her grandfather used for most of his movable toys. Instead, Sadie stared down at an orb full of a thick red liquid.

Everything seemed connected, like veins to a heart. Was it steam powered? As she looked at it, the liquid in the sphere bubbled, and she felt a soft thumping in her hands.

Everything inside the chest chamber moved. Sadie, not knowing what she did or how, stood stock still, watching the movement with focused eyes. She saw where cogs missed the gear and slipped a few notches before gaining traction again. She noticed how the liquid from the core seemed to travel through tubes and wires, causing parts of the legs and arms to spasm and flinch. What had she done? Sadie could do nothing but stare at the inner workings of a machine she knew little about. She didn't remember winding anything up or turning anything on. The red core still sat in her hands. It was as if the heat from her own body was enough to power the core back up.

'He…lp… me…'

Sadie let out a yell, and for the second time that night fell off her stool, dropping the core back into the chest cavity. The stool crashed to the ground, while Sadie scampered back to her feet and pressed her entire body up against the farthest wall from the workbench.

Had she imagined it? The voice that seemed to come out of the automaton's mouth? With eyes wide in shock and surprise, she forced herself to stare at the face as if daring it to do it again.

Its red eyes blinked.

Sadie let out another scream and rushed to the back door. Maybe the Night Watchmen that stopped by earlier were still outside, nearby, and within yelling distance? She didn't care what punishment they threw at her; this was sorcery.

'Help me…' the automaton spoke again.

It's voice more prominent than the first time, a raspy tone of a damaged airway. It sounded like a music box winding down.

'You spoke! You actually spoke…' Sadie said.

Despite her shaking hand on the doorknob, Sadie couldn't bring her body to move any further beyond the workshop. Maybe it was curiosity, or maybe she was just too petrified by the plea hidden behind the mechanical voice.

'Please… help… me…'

'You won't hurt me or anything? Kill me, attack in any way?' Sadie said, her voice low and timid.

She edged closer to the workbench, her eyes still on the automaton's face. It peered at her through unblinking eyes.

'Help me... please...'

'I'll take that as a no...' Sadie said, closing the gap between her and the machine.

The moment she was back in her sitting position on the stool, her hands above the chest cavity, the head turned back to its original positioning, staring up at the ceiling. Sadie's hands shook, her entire body seemed to shake uncontrollably.

'So... you can talk now... a bit. Should make things more interesting... why don't you tell me about yourself?' Sadie said. It was more for her own sake than to get a reply. The automaton said nothing, though it blinked again. A shudder went down Sadie's spine. 'Well, it's obvious you're not from around these parts, are ya?'

'Logical. Far away.'

Sadie fumbled with the screwdriver in her hand. She almost expected to hear it call out for help again. Usually anything with a sound box has a limited range of responses... then again, all she's ever worked with is basic lullabies for music boxes or bird songs for the multiple little bird bots she made.

'Do you have a name?' Talking was the only way for Sadie to calm her shaking hands. It wasn't like there was a lot left to fix, but what still needed her attention also needed her steady and precise hands to finish. 'I've been calling you Cali, but if you have your own name... I can start calling you by that instead?'

'Does not compute.'

'So... you don't have a name? What about a function?'

'Error. Memory not found.'

'Wait, stop... I've got to fix these vocals. I'm not sure about you, but the half mechanical, half musical mix you've got going on is driving me up the wall,' Sadie said with a small smile.

Prying open the neck porcelain plating, she gained access to the music box in her throat. Sure enough, with some fiddling, tinkering, and replacing a few parts, the voice box looked almost brand new.

'Okay, try that...'

'Testing voice enhancement.'

Sadie stared at the doll. She sounded like an actual human being. Well, more as in the voice had the melody, beat and emphasis a human carries. The short, detailed, and mechanical statements she made signified that she clearly was not human.

'Better, right?' Sadie said, turning back to the rest of the body. 'So, let's try this again. You don't remember your name? Do you remember anything from... before?'

'Negative. No name in memory banks.' The automaton blinked and tilted her head towards Sadie. 'Cali is acceptable.'

'Okay... Cali it is.'

What the hell was she doing? Sadie could see the gears trying to work as she spotted the areas that were struggling or failing to keep up with the rest. This thing was speaking to her, intelligently. Understanding everything she said and returning a reply. The automatons she heard about over the wireless were never this complex. They were used mostly for manual labour or repetitive tasks. Or programmed to sing a particular pre-recorded song from a human singer. Sadie never heard of such an automaton like the one she was working on right now. Not even the Grand Masters in Ashrath could have this technology at their disposal.

This was way beyond her expertise. What was she going to do with her? Fix her up and send her back into the world? She would surely break in a fortnight. The Night Watchmen already searched her shop once. How was she going to explain something like Cali during the next inspection? Sadie sighed, realising far too late she should have left well enough alone back in that abandoned factory.

'What... is... your name?'

Sadie blinked, startled by the question now being presented to her. For a heartbeat she didn't answer; it as if she forgot her own name. Looking down at the unusual machine that was now staring back at her, Sadie felt the weight of responsibility fall on her shoulders. Whatever her function, this automaton was different, special even, and worth protecting.

'Ah, it's Sadie... Sadie McLachlan...'

'Thank you, Sadie McLachlan.'

'For what?'

'Saving me.'

The silence that filled the workshop seemed to stretch out for eternity. Sadie's shoulders relaxed. She felt her heart slow down to its normal rhythm and smiled wholeheartedly back at Cali.

'You're welcome.'

*

Sadie awoke late the next morning, hunched over the now empty workbench. The sky outside her window was already full of sun that was shining right into her face. She leaned back and stretched on the stool, rotating her neck back and forth. She could feel the kink still there and just as painful as ever. Sadie made a mental note to use her bedroom up on the second floor more often.

Memories of the previous night slowly filtered through her conscious thoughts. Staring down at the empty workbench, Sadie's heart raced. Where was Cali? Did she move her somewhere, or did the automaton get up and walk away on her own? The last thing Sadie remembered was talking to Cali as she placed the last piece of the porcelain shell overtop of her intricate insides. The two talked constantly that night. Cali's speech was improving with every sentence she heard and spoke. That the automaton seemed to learn sent another uncomfortable shiver down Sadie's spine. However, since awakening, Cali did not show any hostile intentions fitting of a spy from Ashrath.

The automaton's memory was probably the key to this feature. Sadie took only a brief look at the 'brain' of the automaton the previous night; even just the memory of the intricate workings made her head hurt all over again. She didn't even have tools small enough to fit into the openings she saw. It seemed damaged and contained empty slots. Were they intended for room for expansion and growth?

It was beyond Sadie's skill and knowledge to fix Cali's memory, though she briefly remembered mentioning that there might be books in the Tower that could help.

Sadie's stomach churned uncomfortably. She let out a soft groan and searched the workshop once more for the missing automaton, hoping that Cali wasn't stupid enough to go straight into the Grand Master's headquarters by herself. She wasn't anywhere in the workshop or in the apartment above. Sadie returned to the main floor and frantically turned around, biting her nails on one hand while the other scratched her head.

That's when she heard muttering coming from the shop, at the front end of the building, where she sold her work, collected orders and repairs from customers.

'No, she wouldn't have...' Sadie muttered to herself as she tentatively moved towards the single door that separated the business from the workshop.

The muffled voices grew the closer she got. Panic seized Sadie's mind and body. She threw open the door with wide eyes and shaking hands, afraid she'll see people clustered around Cali, tearing her apart while others yelled down the street for the Night Watch.

'Ah, there she is. The last decent clockwork mechanic in the city, if you ask me.'

Sadie blinked, unsure if her mind was imagining things or not. The woman who spoke was elderly, with large grey streaks through her dark hair. She wore a violet dress with some dark-coloured fur around her neck. It was her hat that gave the identity away. It had a large brim and was covered with enough feathers and ribbon that it could almost fly away on its own. Mrs Winston was wife to the chief of the Night Watch. She strutted around town as if she owned the place and was head of the busybody brigade.

'Well? Don't stand there gawking, girl. Wasn't I telling you the other day you needed help? I'm glad you finally took my advice and hired this girl. She's strange, though, definitely not from around here. But with everyone leaving, having those country bumpkins move in to take their places should help Melmoor recover.'

'Hired?' Sadie questioned.

She stepped closer to the counter. She saw the feminine pocket watch sitting delicately on a dark red velvet handkerchief on the glass countertop, with Cali standing next to it, writing a repair slip. Cali wore a dark red with black trimmed pinafore dress with one of Sadie's buttoned up white dress shirts that went all the way up her neck and just briefly touched her chin. It covered all the grooves from the ceramic plates. Her reddish blond hair combed to perfection and fell in neat, wavy locks along her shoulders and down her back.

'Good morning, Sadie McLachlan,' Cali said casually, turning her head slightly towards the open doorway behind her.

'Polite to boot, eh, Sadie?' Mrs Winston said, ignoring the stiff movement of Cali's neck. 'You know, I've worried about you and this shop ever since your precious mother died all those years ago. Tragic, tragic… the illness took far too many precious lives back then…'

Sadie tried to pay attention to Mrs Winston, who jabbered on like no tomorrow. She eyed the shop, noticing a slight uptick in traffic coming in and out. It wasn't like her shelves were full these days. Lately, her income was largely thanks to repairs or custom orders that came in. Though even those barely paid the bills. Yet, somehow, in the first few hours of the day, the repair slots were full, and more people were shuffling through the shop. They were mostly men, and to Sadie's horror, were constantly eyeing Cali. Did they know? Were they gawking? Suspicious?

'Never been the same without them… goodness me, I know you try, child, but you haven't even had the chance to enter the Tower yourself because of the war and your grandfather's failing health,' Mrs Winston continued.

'I passed and received my apprenticeship license,' Sadie said.

Her fingers tapped against the glass countertop. Her eyes continued to dart around the shop and out the windows at the passing crowd. Would those Night Watchmen from last night show up again? What would happen if they spotted Cali?

'Ha, an apprenticeship? You think that's going to keep this place afloat? Eventually the Tower will require you to take the Master exams. I'm surprised they haven't done so yet. Only a Master can own and run a business in Melmoor.'

Sadie's eyes darted back to Mrs Winston. There was a bit of a smirk on that wrinkled face of hers. Was this a threat? Or blackmail?

'As for speaking to you, this pocket watch once belonged to my dear grandmother. Thought I lost it. But lo-and-behold, I was cleaning up our attic and there it was, in the chest with all the old china from my grandmother's house. Never thought it'd show up there. Needs a lot of work though, think you can handle it?'

Blackmail it is. Sadie kept her back straight and glanced down at the ornate object. As much as Mrs Winston claimed this belonged to her departed grandmother, one look told Sadie otherwise. It had the crest of the Hewlett family. The same family that packed up and moved away three months ago.

'Of course. Nothing out of the ordinary. I'll have the watch cleaned and tuned by tomorrow if you like,' Sadie said with the largest and fakest smile she could muster.

This seemed to do it for Mrs Winston, who nodded her head and took out her coin purse to pay the deposit.

'I have filled out the requests of the other orders that have arrived today,' Cali said, gesturing to the small trays of items along the back wall.

'I saw... didn't expect to be so busy today,' Sadie said, still amazed how nobody seemed shocked or surprised at Cali's presence.

At least not in the way she thought they'd act. It was as if they didn't see the jerky motions and thought she was just another human like them.

'The men seemed overly friendly when I opened up this morning,' Cali added.

She ripped the repair sheet off the pad and set it, with the pocket watch, into the repair tray and placed it with the dozen others along the wall behind the counter.

'Men, humph,' Mrs Winston said, with a disapproving shake of her head. 'One pretty face, and they all go mad. You watch yourself, girly. They may be friendly now, but all men are the same deep down. They'll turn on you in a second after dark, or when they think they are alone. Sadie, I hope you're keeping a watchful eye on this new girl of yours. She seems far too innocent to be let loose on the streets.'

'On that, we can agree on, Mrs Winston,' Sadie said with a nod. Cali seemed to stare at the two of them with a tilted head and a perplexing gaze.

'I do not understand.'

'As well you shouldn't. It's not proper for a young woman like yourself to know the wilds of men's hearts. The stories my Colin tells me! Soldiers taking advantage of barmaids and waitresses when passing through town! The shame of them! I'm just glad the Night Watch is out there doing their job. Keeping those hoodlums in check. She's a good one, this Cali of yours. Don't lose her.'

With that, Sadie was glad to wave goodbye as Mrs Winston left the shop. It seemed her presence, and their chat, scared off several men who were just lollygagging around. The shop emptied quickly afterwards, allowing Sadie to lean over the countertop and let out a whimper.

'What were you thinking, Cali? Opening the shop by yourself?'

Sadie turned to face the automaton, who just stared back in that emotionless glare of hers.

'I do not understand. Are you upset about my performance? Did I do something incorrect?'

'I… yes, no… why did you open the shop?'

'You were asleep. I saw the sign that said you opened at nine, so I opened the store at the allocated time.'

'What if someone noticed you?'

'They did. Like I mentioned earlier, the men were friendly.'

'NO! Not in that way! What if anyone recognised you weren't… you know… real?'

'Real?'

Sadie moaned and leaned further over the counter. It was like talking to a child. How was she supposed to explain to Cali the dangers of others learning about her secret? She could be the spy everyone is looking for. Not to mention she was a complete mystery. From her discovery in that old factory, to the odd core that powered her body, to even the fact that she reacted and did tasks of her own desire. If anyone found out the truth, they'd throw her in jail and dismantle Cali.

'Okay, listen,' Sadie took a breath and straightened her back. 'I don't know where you came from. And until we figure out how to solve your memory issue, you don't either. It's obvious you're not from Melmoor, as your maker's mark isn't anything I recognise. So, until we find some answers, promise me you'll stay put.'

'Stay put,' Cali repeated.

'Right. Don't go outside or interact with people if you can help it. Seriously, you may look human... but your speech pattern is still off. It won't take long until someone notices that and starts asking too many questions. Do you understand?'

Cali stared at Sadie, unblinking for what felt like five whole minutes.

'I understand. I am different. It is dangerous. Could end up broken again.'

'Yes, exactly! I want to keep you safe, Cali. I also want to help you find your home. Or even where you came from. Maybe if we find your maker, we can fix your memory,' Sadie said.

She was glad Cali finally understood, but suddenly, speaking everything out loud made an additional weight land on her shoulders. How was she going to do all that and keep her shop running?

'Safe. Home,' Cali's eyes closed at this.

If Sadie didn't know better, it looked as if Cali was trying to find some memory to help.

'Hey, don't hurt yourself there. Tomorrow, I'll head to the Tower. It's the only place with archives of all the maker's marks in Olynana, Ebium — that's the country North of us, and Actis — that's an island kingdom the South,' Sadie said, trying to make a plan that wouldn't get the two caught. 'If you are from around these parts, then the archives should have a record of your Maker and his mark. From there, we'll have a location to focus our search on. Sounds like a plan, right?'

Cali nodded her head, her lips pointed up in a smile. It was odd to watch, eerie even, given how lifelike it looked.

'For now... might as well put you to work. You seem to operate the shop better than I expected. You're a quick learner. If you want to man the counter, I'll start working on these repairs,' Sadie said, grabbing a few trays and taking them to the back.

'Oh,' Sadie paused in the doorway. 'Let me know if anyone gives you a hard time… or asks too many questions… or if you have questions… just be sure to act… as human as possible. Got it?'

'Understood,' Cali said with a nod.

She then turned to face the shop, standing as still as stone, waiting for the next customer to enter.

'Yeah… good…' Sadie muttered under her breath, her voice dripping with sarcasm.

*

The following afternoon, Sadie put on her best pinafore skirt, a dark blue plaid fabric. It was far too puffy for her liking, given that Sadie preferred to stick to the slacks and cotton shirts when working in the shop. However, the Tower wasn't an everyday excursion, and every craftsman and maker in Melmoor knew to dress their best when arriving. Besides the skirt, she had to dig through her mother's chest for a suitable white blouse, which was again way too puffy in the sleeves. The black leather corset was the tough part. Sadie rarely wore anything this snug fitting, however fashion dictated certain silhouettes were all the rage.

Nothing she wore was brand new. The skirt was worn and faded; the blouse was turning yellow from age, and her corset was battered from overuse. Still, looking at herself in the full-length mirror, Sadie had to admit, she looked more like a lady than she normally did.

With her dark brown hair brushed, combed, and pinned

up in a loose bun at the back of her head, Sadie entered the workshop to present herself to Cali, who was polishing up her boots.

'Okay. How do I look? Passable?' Sadie asked, practicing her walk around the workshop in the two-inch heels.

She felt herself tip and weave while trying to keep herself as straight and balanced as possible.

'Beautiful,' Cali said.

'Don't mock me. I feel like I'm pretending to be someone I'm not,' Sadie said, yanking at the collar around her neck. 'Whatever, it'll have to do. You understand the plan?'

'Stay and wait for your return,' Cali nodded her head.

'Yes, well,' Sadie grabbed the piece of paper where she copied Cali's maker's mark onto for her to compare in the archives. 'I hope to be back in a few hours, before dark at the latest. You'll be okay on your own, right?'

'Affirmative.'

'Don't answer the door... don't peek through the windows. If you get bored, there are a few books in the bookcase upstairs...' Sadie looked around the workshop, before landing a worried expression on Cali. 'Be safe, okay?'

'Affirmative,' Cali said, following Sadie to the door. 'Please be careful, Sadie McLachlan.'

Sadie smiled and almost laughed at Cali's face as it mimicked the concern she showed on her own before closing the door between them.

*

The Tower was one of several buildings clustered together in the centre of the city that the Grand Masters used for the tutelage of their many students. Some were dormitories for those who came from out of town, others were workshops, classrooms, and even warehouses to store all their unique inventions. Men and women who wandered between these buildings all wore the same uniform; green jumpers and dresses with black dress shirts for women, and matching green cloaks and black slacks and shirts for men. It was like wearing a badge of honour in the city. Students came from all over Olynana and even beyond its borders to learn at the heels of their Grand Masters.

Sadie climbed the stone steps; the clock tower was now directly overhead. Its ticking seemed to reverberate through her entire body. The only other time she passed through the Tower's archway was to write her apprentice exams three years ago. She felt as nervous then as she was now. The Tower hadn't changed one bit during the war. The white stones still glimmered under the mid-afternoon sun. Even the courtyard was still as lush and full of green trees and beautiful flower beds. And the students still stared down their noses at her as she passed.

It wasn't like she was breaking any rules. The Tower was always open to the public during the day, allowing anyone from any station to enter and learn at their own pace. The money only flowed when one wanted to take classes, exams or become a Master themselves.

Sadie kept her head down and hurried straight to the Archives in the south-west section of the Tower. The attending Master directed Sadie to the section of her inquiry. She wasted no time scouring the leather-bound books for a mark that closely resembled the one etched on Cali's core plate.

Most of the books were just lists compiled together in

alphabetical order. Next to each name was their mark. As with hers and her grandfather's, most of the marks contained letters of the maker's name. Sadie must have stared and searched through a dozen books with no match for hours before she finally leaned back in her chair and gave a heavy sigh of defeat.

'Miss McLachlan?' The elderly Master's voice filled the silence around Sadie.

She rubbed her eyes and stared up at the large glass window behind her to see the streaks of gold and red of the setting sun.

'Yes, I'm finished here... I'll be leaving shortly,' Sadie said.

She expected the woman to kick her out now that the Archives and most of the Tower's buildings were closing down for the day.

'Grand Master Larkin would like to see you before you leave.'

Sadie stopped in her tracks. She was just piling up the books she was looking at when the name of the Head of the Grand Masters flooded out of the woman's lips.

'Excuse me? I... there must be some mistake?' Sadie said, her heart pounded loudly in her chest. 'It's late, I need to make it back home before curfew... send my regards...'

'No one ever refuses an offer of tea from the Grand Masters.'

Sadie gulped. Several thoughts went through her head at once, each more frightening than the other. First, she wondered if she did something wrong. Had the rules changed on her? Were the Archives suddenly off limits to the public? Then she recalled Mrs Winston's blackmail about not being allowed to run a shop without a Master license. Finally, and most dreadful of all, Sadie remembered Cali and feared they learned of her secret automaton.

'You look as white as a sheet, girl. There is nothing to worry about. Grand Master Larkin would only like to have tea with you. He does with random students all the time.'

'But I'm not a student.'

'You are Avery McLachlan's granddaughter. I'm sure the Grand Master only wants to catch up and make sure you are doing okay during these turbulent times.'

All Sadie could do was smile politely and nod her head. There was no running away now. She saw the large cannons that surrounded the turrets of the Tower's openings. The Night Watchmen lingered around with large guns on their shoulders that she had never seen before. Sadie didn't want to find out what other weapons the Grand Master and their students were working on secretly for the military. She heard stories of Zadock Royden Larkin, head of the Grand Masters. He has final say on what is priority on research and innovation in the Tower. It was his ultimate word that created the Night Watch, and his order that most likely had Cali shot down and accused of as the spy they were all looking for.

The woman led Sadie to the centre of the tower, where an iron gate and door opened for them. She entered the lift, only ever seeing it in the past. The doors closed with a hissing sound, and small pillows of steam filled the doorway for a split second before the lift rumbled to life.

Sadie grabbed on to the railing inside her little metal box with white knuckles as the lift rose upward at an alarming speed. Any attempt to prepare herself before being introduced to the Head of the Grand Masters went out the window the moment the lift rose into the air and up the spire of the Tower itself.

A minute later, the doors opened, and the iron gate swung

back. Sadie took a tentative step out of the lift and almost collapsed into the oval-shaped corridor she found herself in. A green and gold rug filled most of the floor, along with several oil paintings of portraits of past Grand Masters that lined the surrounding walls. Before her were three doors. However, the woman below didn't mention which door to enter. Maybe she could slip out before Larkin could discover she was even here in the first place?

Sadie turned back to the lift, but the doors closed right in her face. A panel of small electric light bulbs above the doorway glowed one by one. She quickly realised the lift had returned to the ground floor.

A creak of a door opening caused Sadie to yelp in surprise and jump around to face the man who appeared in the doorway directly opposite of the lift. She felt her cheeks warm with embarrassment as she quickly bowed to the Head of the Grand Masters. Then, Sadie quickly remembered she was a woman and tried to turn her bow into a curtsey halfway through, with disastrous results.

'Grand Master Larkin... it's a pleasure...' Sadie sputtered out, her tongue getting in the way.

She looked up at the man. He was an old, wrinkly fellow with a long greying beard that almost hit the floor. He wore circular spectacles with a second pair of goggles on top of his head, with multiple magnifying lenses attached and sprawled out like spider legs.

'Ah, yes, Miss McLachlan. Good, good, I'm glad Bertha caught you before you left for the evening,' the old man said.

There was a smile on his lips, which took Sadie aback. She expected some crusty old geezer, not some friendly old sage.

'Come, come, I've got our tea ready. I also had the kitchen staff send up some sweets too. Can't have tea without sweets, eh? I'm sure spending all that time in the archives this afternoon gave you a bit of an appetite?'

'Ah… thank you, sir,' Sadie said as the old man just about pulled her through the opened doorway.

The wedged shaped room had three narrow windows overlooking the city. Sadie couldn't help but walk towards the windows to look down at Melmoor. She had never seen the city from this height before. The view was spectacular. She could see the artisan's streets to the North, the train station to the East, and a small glance of the port and river to the South.

Besides the view, he decorated the room with exotic rugs of all different shapes and patterns in shades of blue, violet, gold and silver. Bookcases lined most of the southern wall, while on the opposite side was a desk covered in papers. A workbench stood off to the side of the desk with shelves full of bottles filled with unknown and colourful thick liquids.

'Sit, sit, you can marvel at my collection while you have your tea,' Larkin said.

He escorted Sadie towards the middle of the room where a round coffee table stood, covered with everything for tea. Several types of furniture surrounded the coffee table: a sofa, an overstuffed chair, and two ornate high-back chairs. Sadie was about to go towards the sofa when Larkin pulled her towards the high-back chair instead. It was not uncomfortable, but it forced Sadie to sit tall and straight, which only added to her stress.

'So, tell me more about yourself. How is the McLachlan shop holding up? Still doing business?' Larkin asked, pouring tea into two bone china teacups, each painted with a rose pattern.

'Ah... I'm sorry?' Sadie said, surprised by the subtle question about the business of the shop.

Her heart pounded. Was this about operating the shop without a Master's License?

'The shop, the shop. How are you handling yourself now that your grandfather has passed?' Larkin pressed, handing her a teacup.

Sadie took it, but saw her outstretched arms shake uncontrollably. She tried to remain calm, but despite the pleasantness of Larkin's voice, his beady blue eyes seemed to pierce into her soul.

'It's still holding up,' Sadie answered.

'Good, good...' Larkin said, his voice trailing away, yet his eyes never seemed to leave her face. 'You never returned after receiving your apprenticeship license. I had hoped you'd follow in your grandfather's path. Join the Tower and become an official Master yourself.'

Was this a question or a statement?

'That was the original plan, but you know... with everything going on, the situation changed,' Sadie answered, trying to sound just as casual as Larkin.

'That they do,' Larkin sighed and nodded his head understandingly. His eyes finally dropped, and Sadie's shoulders dropped as some tension left her body. Maybe that was all there was to it? 'Still, with your grandfather now deceased, it is only natural you return and finish your studies. Correct? Earn yourself a Master Certificate and keep the shop in the family.'

'Excuse me?' Sadie looked up, startled at the hidden message behind his words. She blinked a few times, afraid if she said the wrong thing, he would in that exact moment tear the shop she held dear to her heart away. With the war, and the lack of funds, there was no way she could take the exams or even the required classes to receive her Master's certificate. 'I'm sorry… you must have misunderstood my intentions for my visit today. I don't have the time, nor even the money at my disposal, to advance my status.'

'Oh, I see… that is problematic, isn't it?' Larkin said. His voice sounded finite and void of any emotional understanding. His posture changed, too. Instead of leaning back in the opposite chair, he sat straight, his blue eyes once more staring Sadie down into submission. 'I must ask, what brought you through the Tower's doors today?'

Sadie took the strategic approach to stuff one of the bite-size cakes into her mouth to prevent her from answering right away. She could tell him the truth. After all, he was Head Grand Master and may know more Maker's Marks in the world. It would save a lot of time in the archives. However, she had to phrase things carefully. Cali's existence was in jeopardy here.

'Well, I found a strange Maker's Mark on one of the… clocks… that came into my shop the other day,' Sadie swallowed the cake and gave Larking an innocent look. 'I was merely curious who made the clock… it was in pretty poor condition, and you know, with my apprentice status, there are still things I've yet to learn. The clock has given me a few frustrating nights.'

'Ah… perhaps I can be of some assistance then?'

Sadie drank half her tea in one gulp. Larkin did not sound curious. It was as if he expected her to say the words she did. Once again, Sadie's heart pounded in her chest. Could she bluff her way out of this? The more she hesitated, the more she could sense Larkin's eyes bare into her mind and soul. It was like watching a cat prepared to pounce. Sadie tried to stay calm, reaching slowly into her pouch at her waist to pull the slip of paper out.

Larkin grabbed the paper the moment he saw it in her hand. Sadie couldn't even react in time, even if she wanted to. He was on his feet and standing to her right within seconds of her arm moving to her side. She glanced up at the imposing Grand Master as he unfolded the paper and stared at the mark with wide, unblinking eyes. She couldn't help but tremble at the sight of him. There was an overwhelming sensation to flee the room, that somehow this mark was far worse than she could ever imagine. Sadie placed the teacup and saucer down on the coffee table, preparing to excuse herself immediately from Larkin's presence, when his voice split the uncomfortable silence.

'Where did you get this mark?' Larkin's eyes were no longer on the paper, but set fully on Sadie's face.

'Ah, like I said... from a clock that came into my shop.'

Sadie hoped she sounded confident, but she couldn't get rid of that high, questionable pitch that came at the end of her statement.

'This is not a mark from our Tower. This isn't even a mark from a Maker,' Larkin pressed on.

He moved back across the coffee table and opened a box she hadn't noticed before, hidden behind the teapot and the tray of sweets. There was an unnatural buzz sound as he pressed a button hidden in the box. Before Sadie could figure out what happened, arm bands emerged from the chair she sat in, locking her wrists down.

'What the... what is the meaning of this?' Sadie asked,

struggling against the restraints.

'Do you know what this mark is? Who it belongs to?' Larkin asked as he leaned down towards Sadie. There was a crazed look on his face. Sadie tried to back away, but locked to the chair, all she could do was shake her head. 'An alchemist!'

'An alchemist?' Sadie repeated.

A dawning realisation filled her mind. Could that be the secret behind Cali's core? It wasn't mechanical at all... but magic from an alchemist?

'Where did you get this mark? What sort of device has landed in your shop?' Larkin said, his voice louder and harsher.

His act of being a benevolent Grand Master disappeared, replaced by the tyrannical man the rumours around the city mentioned.

'I... well... it's a complicated piece of machinery...' Sadie said, still for the life of her trying to bluff her way out of this mess. Maybe if she stuck with her story, he'd calm down and let her go? 'Now that you mentioned alchemy, that explains a lot of the problems I'm having.' Sadie forced a smile, though her hands still struggled against the straps that now dug tighter into her skin. 'It's getting late, sir... I'm afraid I don't have the answers you're looking for... and if I'm to get home before curfew...'

'Do you know the chair you're sitting in was once used by the Inquisition? Way back in the day, it was used to get confessions out of the sinners. This piece is an antique, and it still seems to work. Whenever someone tells a lie, the straps get tighter. Tell me, McLachlan, how tight are those straps?' Larkin's voice was calm as he strode around the room, not caring that he was torturing someone at all.

This was what made Sadie's heart plummet into her

stomach. The casualness he took to the pain she felt. The fear was plastered on her face as she squirmed and wiggled against the tight restraints.

'Let us try this again, and this time be honest, McLachlan. You do not want to see how tight these restraints can go,' Larkin warned. 'What came into your shop? What did you discover that had this mark on it?'

'I don't know! A clock of some kind!' Sadie said and immediately yelled out in pain.

The restraints had dug into the surface of her skin, through the blouse, and now she could see a small trail of blood seeping out and staining the cuffs.

'Liar!' Larkin shouted, pointing to the blood seeping through. 'Look at all I've done for Melmoor and the country of Olynana as well! Haven't I kept you safe? Protected by the weapons we develop and create here? Haven't I?'

Larkin's face was bright red, his eyes wide, which filled Sadie with fright. All she could do was nod her head as tears streamed down her face.

'Then why lie to me, dear? Why prevent me from protecting you? Do you want to lose your hands? Do you want me to close McLachlan shop permanently? I know you are running your grandfather's shop without the proper license and certificate. Don't deny it. I've allowed you to work unpunished because of the respect I had towards your grandfather. I hoped that he'd send you to the Tower before his death… but I see I was mistaken. You seem to be just as headstrong as he was.'

'Don't talk about my grandfather! If you really respected him, you wouldn't be torturing his granddaughter,' Sadie spat.

'This isn't torture. I am getting the truth! I am protecting the innocents of Melmoor. You, my dear, are doing this to yourself by refusing to help me. This mark you found. It belongs to an Alchemist by the name of Lionel Amos Silver. You can see the flourished L and S in the mark,' Larkin said, holding up the paper and tracing the letters Sadie never even noticed. 'A remarkable alchemist, always inventing and meddling in places he doesn't belong. Tales of his inventions travelled all over the world, along with his disregard for the natural order of things. He was just that, a name on the wind. That was until our spies discovered he was working for Ashrath. Hired, or imprisoned, you never know with those people. Either way, he was building weapons unlike anything we could ever imagine. Weapons with unbreakable shells that looked exactly like us. Able to move and talk like a human but programmed to locate and destroy targets. Mechanical Assassins.'

Sadie's chest seemed to contract. Her heart pounded heavily in her ears. Her body trembled, and she stared at the crazed look in Larkin's eyes. All of her worst fears were coming to the surface. Cali's unusual design, the tough as nails porcelain casing, the red glowing core, and the quick learning capabilities.

'You, Sadie, are blocking our path to victory. By withholding vital information on this weapon, you are damning us all to death! Ashrath's secret weapon will destroy us, Melmoor, and Olynana if you continue to hide this doll from us.'

'She's not a weapon!' Sadie shouted, gripping the wooden arms of the chair tightly.

She didn't care about her hands. This cannot be Cali's function.

'Don't let her demeanour fool you, girl! She will kill you if given the chance. It is your duty to hand her over, help us unlock Lionel's secrets, and with that knowledge we can turn the ceasefire on its head. There would be no more need for peace talks! We will show them our might, our superiority!'

'You're wrong! Wrong about everything!' Sadie shouted back. 'I'll never give her up to someone like you. I don't care what you say, or believe, it's all wrong. I know her, I know she's not what you claim to be.'

In that moment, as the words finished leaving Sadie's lips, the entire Tower shook around them. It felt like an earthquake had ruptured the entire city. Dust fell from the ceiling, and for a split second Sadie thought her chair would fall on its side. There was a rumble and out of nowhere a shock wave hit the tower, blasting out every single glass panel in the room. Sadie felt shards of glass whip by her face. Larkin fell back as the blast behind forced him to the ground.

Sadie took advantage of the distraction and lowered her head to her right hand and tried to fish out one of the several bobby-pins that held her hair in place. She realised there was a lock mechanism under the arm of the chair while Larkin was raging about the alchemist. She could pick the lock and loosen the restraints. Or try to, at least.

'We're under attack!' Larkin shouted, getting to his feet. Sure enough, billows of large black smoke filtered up from the ground and past the broken windows. 'The weapon is loose! It's here to kill us all!'

Sadie could see the madness spread over Larkin's face as his eyes, now wide with fear, frantically darted about the room. His hair seemed to stick up like a frightened cat. Then at once, as if sanity resumed, his ice-cold eyes fell on her.

'You! It is you she wants. It is you who sent her, isn't it?!'

'No!' Sadie replied, and felt the straps dig further into her wrists.

'I will destroy that weapon if it is the last thing I do!' Larkin said, rushing towards his desk and pushing a pile of old papers aside.

Sadie watched him, while desperately trying to pick the lock with little success. He lifted a wired cone-shaped receiver off the desk. He shouted words into it, and after a pause, a voice travelled back through the cone, making it audible to the entire room.

'It's a girl... but it can't be. Nothing seems to damage it.' The male voice over the cone device said. 'It keeps asking for someone... and... oh my god...'

'What is it?' Larkin shouted.

'She's climbing the tower! Sir! She's heading towards your window.'

'I want every available guard, soldier and student armed to the teeth and up here in seconds! We cannot let Ashrath's assassin defeat us!'

'Cali...' Sadie said in a low whisper.

Her eyes grew just as wide as Larkin's as they shared a knowing stare between each other. What was Cali doing here? She's going to get captured, destroyed! Could she really be after her?

'There, you see! This monstrosity of a machine is about to kill us both. What do you think about her now? Still want to protect her?'

'You bet I do!' Sadie said, without hesitation.

In that moment, a figure landed on the windowsill. The dark colours of the sunset silhouetted the feminine shape. All Sadie and Grand Master Larkin could see was the blood-red eyes that seemed to glow out of the darkness.

'Devil!' Larkin shouted.

Cali ignored the old man and walked directly over to Sadie. 'You're in danger.'

With that statement, the automaton bent her head down at the restraints, grabbed the two metal bands and ripped them off of Sadie's wrists. Freed, Sadie rushed to the door and into the hallway, Cali followed on her heels. Larkin hunched under his desk, his eyes trailing the two as they crossed his room.

'You shouldn't have come!' Sadie said, punching the button next to the lift doors. She eyed the light bulbs above, as they slowly blinked floor by floor upwards towards them. 'Larkin is going to tear you apart! They think you're an assassin, or a weapon... or... I don't want that to happen to you!'

'You're in danger,' Cali replied in her typical causal style voice.

The two heard shouts echoing up from the spiral staircase next to the lift. It seemed Larkin's reinforcements were on the way. Sadie pushed Cali back into Larkin's room and slammed the door closed, trapping them inside with the Grand Master.

'Nowhere to go,' Larkin said. 'This is your last chance, McLachlan. Hand over the enemy's device now and all will be forgiven. I'd even give you an honorary Master's certificate so you can keep running your family's shop without further hassle.'

'I told you before, I'm never going to hand Cali over to the likes of you!' Sadie said, pulling Cali towards the window.

It was a large drop. It amazed her that Cali could climb it at all.

'You are in danger, Sadie McLachlan.'

'I know!' Sadie shouted, tears streaming down her face. Larkin stood next to his desk, the cone receiver, or talking device, still in his hand as he shouted orders to those on the ground. 'I'm sorry... I don't know how to get out of this...'

'Do you trust me?' Cali asked.

Startled by the question, Sadie turned to see Cali stare deeply into her face. Even Larkin seemed distracted by the unusual question it posed.

'Yes, I do...' Sadie said, though she couldn't help but hesitate a little. 'What...'

Before she could ask her question, Cali's hands wrapped around her waist and pulled her out the window with her.

Sadie screamed as the ground rushed up towards her. It was the lift experience all over again, but this time in reverse. She closed her eyes and held on to Cali's body, expecting to feel the guttural crunch when they landed on cobblestones. Instead, Cali positioned herself under Sadie, moving her to her back as the ground approached. There was still a crunch, but for Sadie there was no pain, and no bright light of the afterlife. Opening her eyes, she saw the large crater-like dent Cali made upon landing in the courtyard of the Tower. She could see the cracks and fissures spread out along the road and up the nearby buildings like a spider web. The Night Watch, students, and military soldiers scampered around as the dust settled.

'She's over here!' someone nearby yelled.

Sadie slid off Cali's back and pulled her out of the crater and towards the streets just as another yell of, 'Take Aim!'

Cali pushed Sadie behind the corner of the nearest building just as a hail of bullets rained in from the sky. Sadie watched with wide-eyed wonderment as each bullet bounced off of Cali's tough shell exterior. She knew it was tough, but to withstand a bullet was not what she expected. The bullet fire stalled before Sadie heard the hum of the cannons on the turret come to life.

Sadie had only heard the cannons on one other occasion, back near the beginning of the war, when Ashrath's troops were trying to invade the city. It was a sound she would never forget. She pulled Cali into the alleyway just as a bright blue line of electrical energy emitted out of the cannon towards their location. Sadie felt the blazing energy burn around her skin as she fell to the ground. Within seconds, all that remained of their hiding spot was a pile of smouldering ruins. The shock wave shook the ground and nearby buildings as walls around them crumbled and deteriorated. She looked up to see Cali hunched over her, taking the brunt of the damage herself.

Her body remained intact, undamaged from the blast. Only the clothes she wore were burnt and torn. Could Larkin be right after all? Was Cali nothing more than a weapon bent on destroying her target?

'Sadie McLachlan, are you injured?' Cali asked, staring down at her bloodied cuffs. 'You did not return as planned. I grew worried. Afraid.'

The concern on the automaton's face reminded Sadie of the truth. How could some machine created for war worry about others?

'I'm okay… but what about you? That was some hit you took.'

'Negative. I'm fully operational.'

'That's for sure…' Sadie said in a grim tone. 'But why are you here? I told you to stay at the shop!'

'Curfew has begun. You were still not home, and I remembered.'

'Remembered?'

But Sadie didn't have time to get a response. She heard shouts and orders from the Night Watch, who reorganised themselves and were ready to go on the offensive again. Students from the Tower joined as well, working hand in hand with the Night Watch. Peering out from the battered wall, she could see large, cannon shaped weapons being brought out from the warehouses. These weapons were unlike anything Sadie had ever seen before. Going by the symbols along the sides, she knew they were intended for front line military assaults.

'We'll have to finish this conversation later. We've got to get out of here and to safety, fast,' Sadie said, eyeing their surroundings for an escape route.

Every direction was blocked, either by debris, students, or the Night Watch. Getting away won't be easy.

'Affirmative,' Cali said with a nod.

'Hey, wait, what…' Sadie said as she felt Cali's arms grab her around the waist for the second time and lift her into the air.

Cali jumped over ten feet, landing directly onto one of the nearby roofs. Before she could catch her breath, Cali jumped once more to another rooftop. The two continued from rooftop to rooftop until the sounds from the Tower's courtyard faded from earshot. It took them minutes to cross the city and land in the alley next to McLachlan's Clockworks.

'Enough! No more jumping around!' Sadie said, falling to her knees, panting hard and feeling like she was about to vomit.

'Apologies. It was the only escape route open.' Cali said, bending down to pat Sadie on the back. 'We are safe. We are home.'

'Not for long,' Sadie sighed.

There was no way Larkin was going to take this lying down. Soon the entire Night's Watch, along with the Masters from the Tower and military, would close in around the shop. Cali wasn't a secret anymore, and Larkin seemed obsessed to get his hands on her. How long did they have?

'Quick, we've got to pack and get out of town as fast as possible before they track us down. I don't even want to know what they'll do to you.'

Sadie rushed around the shop and apartment, packing clothes and tools into a couple of leather hide backpacks. Her apprentice license and the last family photo she had of her grandfather and mother were the two most valuable things she still owned. One would allow her to work anywhere while on the run, the other was the only keepsake she could take with her on the run. She folded and stashed the two pieces of paper into her coat pocket next to her heart. With Cali's help, they were in and out of the shop in under ten minutes.

They didn't pause or think about their actions. All Sadie cared about was getting Cali out of Melmoor. As much as she hated the sensation, she allowed Cali to use her impressive jumping and agility to use the rooftops to arrive at the train station in mere minutes. It was much faster than on foot, and out of sight of those on the streets searching for them.

By some luck of the gods, the Night Watch had not reached the train station yet, nor had any warrant or travel ban reached the ticket master's window. Sadie managed a last-minute purchase for two tickets out of Melmoor on the next steam locomotive. It was due to leave seconds after their arrival.

As the train pulled out of the station, Sadie's shoulders sagged in relief. She leaned back in the cushioned seat of the train car.

She never expected the day would end in such calamity. She was forced to abandon her grandfather's shop and flee Melmoor, the only home she ever knew, as a fugitive. A pain tore through her heart. After everything she did to keep her grandfather's shop open, one simple action of fixing a broken automaton destroyed all her hopes and dreams.

'I remembered,' Cali said again.

It seemed she too sensed that most of the danger was now growing more distant behind them.

'What did you remember?' Sadie said.

She didn't look at Cali; her eyes only had the sight of Melmoor and the life she was leaving behind.

'The Tower is dangerous. When you did not return on schedule, I grew concerned, worried. That's when I remembered… being at the Tower is dangerous. I did what someone programmed me to do.'

'Destroy your enemy?' Sadie said without thinking. Only a heartbeat later did her eyes turn to face Cali's. 'I'm sorry, I didn't mean it, honest.'

'I protect,' Cali said in a firm tone.

'Protect what?'

'That, I still cannot remember,' Cali's eyes fell to her lap. 'I did not mean to cause you trouble. The ones at the Tower would not let me in. I tried to call out your name… but they attacked. I had to protect you. But I did not kill anyone.'

That was of little comfort to Sadie.

'I discovered your maker's name. An alchemist named Lionel Amos Silver. Ring a bell?'

'Negative.'

Sadie sighed. It was too good to hope that Cali would

remember the name of her maker. With only a name, it was going to be a long journey to find out where this Silver guy lived.

'You should not have to look after me,' Cali said, her red eyes glancing over at the blood still stained on Sadie's cuffs. 'Because of me, you've lost everything you hold dear. You should not have found me.'

It wasn't the first time Sadie had those thoughts, but hearing it come from Cali only made the weight on her shoulders heavier. Hearing those words made her remember the sacrifice she just gave up, yet at the same time the teachings of her grandfather; *we fix things that are broken*. One look at Cali, and Sadie knew she couldn't be upset with her, nor the choices she made that led her to giving up her life in Melmoor. Grand Master Larkin was wrong. Cali wasn't a secret assassin. Whatever secrets Lionel Silver put into Cali's head and core had to be kept safe. It was now up to Sadie to keep Cali safe until she found the answers to all her questions.

'You might be right, but I'm glad I did,' Sadie said, giving Cali a soft smile. She meant the words from the bottom of her heart. 'We'll find your Maker, Cali. I promise you; I won't stop searching until we uncover the answers to your hidden secrets.'

Sadie glanced back out the window at the last sight of the Tower as it disappeared from view. It was true. Melmoor was not the picturesque city it used to be.

More Precious Than Gold
by Linton Valdock

'Remind me again why we are on the roof of a moving train!' Gilbert Penn shouted.

He was desperately fighting against the buffeting wind as it incessantly tried to wrench his brown derby hat from his pudgy, prematurely balding head. Sweat was pouring down his face; a combination of the stress of his situation and the unrelenting desert heat. He was crawling, or trying to, struggling ahead with a free hand or shuffling a knee forward whenever it didn't feel like he was going to be flung from the train.

At the other end of the train car, strolling arm in arm as if unaffected by both the assault of the wind or the jostling motions of the train, were the man and woman that had come to be Gilbert's travelling companions of late. The man looked over his shoulder, doing something of a double take at Gilbert. He was surprised to see him so far back.

'Do hurry up, man,' Jerome Saint-Earl demanded with a casual tone.

He had a strange accent. It was almost British with hints of French, perhaps, and maybe something from the far east; Gilbert couldn't decide, and he was certainly no expert in the realm of sociolinguistics. To his Midwest ear, everyone from the east coast sounded like pretentious pricks, and everyone from the west coast sounded like a bunch of hicks. Whatever the case, Jerome did not sound like any sort of hick and was a little too amiable to be labelled a pretentious prick.

'I told you before we boarded the train; we've an appointment with my friend Peter at 2.15pm,' Jerome flashed a wide toothy smile, framed by his thick black handlebar moustache. The high afternoon sun glinted off of his round, dark amber sunglasses. 'It's nine minutes after two,' he added after a glance down at his gold pocket watch. 'He should be along any moment now.'

'I assumed there would be a stop,' Gilbert shouted back.

Jerome laughed heartily at this.

'No, of course not, my silly fellow. There are no stops between Mexicali and Los Algodones.'

As a frontier journalist, Gilbert had grown used to following desperados into dangerous situations with little explanation, but the top of a speeding train was new for him. Mostly, he had found himself dodging bullets while fleeing on horseback or crouched behind more than his fair share of overturned tables in the middle of barroom brawls and shootouts. Tales of adventure in the wild west were very popular in the papers on the east coast, and the most popular of these stories were of the outlaws and gunslingers. Gilbert had no trouble finding men and women of questionable character who were more than eager to be potentially immortalised as he chronicled their tales. Inevitably, these lawless name-seekers would fall victim to another of the same ilk. Gilbert would simply move on to the new quick draw or bruiser, giving them the same promises of printed glory and fame.

The last such individual that Gilbert had been travelling with for several weeks was a robber of banks by the name of William "Billy the Bullet" Slapwater. Billy had, rightfully, called Jerome Saint-Earl a cheat during a high-stakes game of cards but made the error of calling him out into the street for a good old fashioned showdown. Unfortunately for The Bullet, he had brought a mere six-shooter to what turned out to be a plasma rifle fight. The large hole in Billy's corpse was still smoking when Gilbert approached Mr Saint-Earl. Persons of such technical savvy, or at least in possession of such inventive technology, were few and far between, especially out here in the west. Such advanced contraptions were far more common in Europe, but things were still pretty raw out here in the west of the Americas. Gilbert could not pass up the opportunity to make more of a name for himself chronicling the travels of a man such as Mr Saint-Earl.

Jerome had initially laughed at the proposition, but over a couple of drinks back in the saloon, he agreed to let Gilbert tag along with him. He warned the reporter, with a smiling wink, that he would be in for a far grander story than what he might hope for. Gilbert could hardly see the harm of a bigger story.

Gilbert had half expected a man like Mr Saint-Earl to demand a contract or some sort of release form, but a simple handshake sealed the deal. Unlike the others that Gilbert had followed around, Jerome was a man of refinement. If his wide, silver, silk tie was not enough of a hint of this, the rest of his well-tailored, monochrome garb was. His long grey woollen overcoat with a wide grey velvet collar perfectly matched the colour of his silk vest as well as his trousers and shoes. Even his low crowned, felt, riding top hat was the same shade of grey. Only his shirt was of a contrasting colour, a deep midnight blue. His hands were adorned with silver rings on all but his thumbs, and each ring was encrusted with several white diamonds. The ring on the third finger of his left hand had one sizeable blue gemstone that glowed with an inner luminance. The stone in the ring was identical to one adorning the pin in his tie. Gilbert found the two glowing stones very distracting. His eyes were constantly drawn down whenever he conversed with the man.

More distracting still was Jerome's cane. Nearly the entire length looked to be made of brass. Not quite midway down, there was a dark-stained wooden grip. Between this and the handle of the cane was a tightly wound copper coil. Three thin brass-looking tubes poked out of the copper coiling near the wooden grip. These flared out to one inch thick, running up the cane's remaining length, becoming thinner again as they curved back into a steel ring just below the handle. Round ended, glass-filled cutaways in the three tubes revealed they contained a brightly glowing, swirling, green gas. The cane's handle was polished ebony, carved into the form of a raven perched upon a ram's skull. Just at the bird's feet protruded what looked like an arcing brass feather.

Jerome claimed to be a master alchemist and inventor. He asserted to Gilbert that the cane's brass-looking portions were actually made of a much stronger alloy of his own concoction. He called the metal rewarium. This included the protruding feather, which was, in fact, a trigger. Jerome's cane also happened to be the plasma rifle that burned a four-inch hole through Billy the Bullet's chest.

'That should be him now.' Jerome pointed his cane towards the northern horizon.

'Who? Where?'

Gilbert was baffled. More accurately, his mind was too preoccupied with not being flung from the train to devote any energy to processing much of anything else.

'Oh, honestly, Jerome, can't you see? The poor man is terrified.'

Jerome's companion, Lady Elena Saphuthest, casually released his arm and strolled back down the train car toward Gilbert. Despite the desert heat here on the Arizona Territory border, she was wholly clad; not a spot of skin could be seen.

Though this might sound suitably modest, her appearance would have been considered quite scandalous, even for the roof of a moving train. For Gilbert, watching her approach was a welcome distraction.

Though she had been wearing a proper full-length dress earlier, just before heading to the exterior of the train, she had discarded the entire skirt with a few quick flips of some well-concealed buttons at her waist. This left her lower half shockingly covered in nothing more than some voluminous bloomers tucked into her rugged, knee-high, tan leather boots. Lady Saphuthest was thin but curvaceous. Her outline was all the more exaggerated by her tightly bound lavender, silk corset bodice.

She reached out a dark purple leather-gloved hand to Gilbert, trying to get him to stand up. When he and Jerome had met up with Lady Saphuthest in San Diego, Gilbert had a suspicion her elbow-length gloves were concealing a prosthetic arm, or maybe two. Whenever she moved, he could faintly hear the telltale clicks and whirs of geared mechanisms. He had been struggling ever since to find a polite way to ask to see them.

They had to be quite sophisticated compared to the bulky, piston-laden tubes and gear monstrosities that Gilbert had seen on occasion in the past. One man, who he had the chance to follow for a short time, had a small, retractable Gatling gun mounted inside his mechanical arm. That adventure had not ended pleasantly. Such rudimentary prosthetics were prone to malfunction, so adding a fully automatic weapon to one had not been the best idea.

Grabbing her left hand now seemed to confirm his suspicions. Her grip was hard and unyielding beneath the leather, and she was startlingly strong. She hoisted Gilbert to his feet with an effortless tug. Gilbert let out a yelp of surprise as he flailed with his other arm, desperately trying to find his balance. She waited only a moment for him to steady himself before leading him by the hand down the length of the car.

'You'll be fine. Come along. You'll need to gather yourself as I expect there may be some running involved.'

She looked back at Gilbert, whose eyes had grown wide with horror at the prospect of trying to do anything more atop this jostling roof. Though she tried, her face offered no comforting expression. Such empathy was concealed behind a double layer of veils. A red and gold beaded face veil covered all but her eyes. Her eyes were obscured by a red lace mourning veil that draped the length of her face and was delicately attached to her black pillbox hat. The billowing of the lace veil in the wind made it all the more difficult to discern any of her features, even as close as Gilbert was then.

Jerome was giving his thick black moustache a contemplative stroke. His eyes were fixed on a distant point in the sky just above the horizon, where a small black dot was quickly growing.

'I hope we won't have to move up a car. It's clear that Gil isn't going to be up to making a jump,' he snickered, shooting Gilbert and Elena a sideways glance as they made their way up the length of the car towards him.

The wind whipped Jerome's long coat wildly about him.

By the time Gilbert and Elena reached Jerome, the object in the sky was clearly visible. It was an airship of some manner, but unlike any of the dirigible balloons Gilbert was used to seeing. The shape of it was like a seafaring vessel, but with an extremely exaggerated width. Like such a vessel, it had enormous paddle wheels on either side. The paddles retracted on the upswing and extended on the downswing to scoop the air. Thick white steam trailed behind it as though it was an enormous mobile cloud factory. It moved remarkably fast and manoeuvred itself in a large arc to align itself with the train approaching from the rear.

'Never met a man as punctual as Peter,' Jerome chuckled.

He was pointing at the ship again with his cane, as if it might be unclear to whom or what he was referring to. It was precisely 2.15pm as the airship lined itself up with the tracks.

'I suspect the train might even be running a little fast today.'

At first, it seemed to Gilbert, the crew of the ship must have miscalculated their trajectory. By the time the craft was above the tracks, it was well behind the train. The gap between the airship and the train, however, was quickly diminishing. Gilbert was struck with an anxiety that overwhelmed the stress he was already feeling from maintaining his balance.

'If… if my understanding is clear, you are expecting us to board that vessel?' Gilbert stammered as he looked at Jerome.

'Not afraid of flying too, are you? I thought you were some sort of adventurer.'

Jerome gave Gilbert a playful slap on the shoulder that sent Gilbert into a short fit of hyperventilating panic, adding to the struggle to maintain his balance. Elena's mechanically rigid grip kept him from going anywhere and was becoming an increasing comfort to Gilbert.

'I don't think I'll have the strength to climb a ladder.'

What if they don't have a ladder? What if they just throw down ropes? These thoughts flooded Gilbert's mind as he replied. Another wave of panic vibrated up his spine. Jerome didn't respond; he just smiled knowingly and pointed again with his cane.

Gilbert turned to see that the ship had already caught up to the train, centred just ten feet above it and just a few cars away from them. A moment later, it was hovering above them. Three ringed, riveted, telescopic tubes, two feet in diameter each, protruded several feet from the ship's base. They were intricately articulated, snaking and stretching about like great mechanical tentacles. Each was capped with a large glass lens and an enormous gaping metal pincer coated in black rubber.

The ship was truly enormous. By Gilbert's estimation, the ship was well over eighty feet wide, not counting the two twelve-foot-wide paddle wheels, and no less than five hundred feet long. Small circles dotted the underside. Gilbert deduced that they were ports for more of the mechanical arms that appeared to be reaching out for him and his companions. Gilbert flinched as one of the large lenses drew in close, nearly skimming the brim of his hat. It took him a moment to realise that the startled looking face within the large glass eye was his reflection.

Jerome leaned in a little to the lens approaching him, giving it a slight tip of his hat.

'Open up, you ol' air dog!' he shouted with a wide smile.

Just then, something caught the corner of his eye, and his smile faded. There was another black dot above the horizon, far off to the south.

'These things aren't going to nab us, are they?' Gilbert asked, leaning back a little from the lens in his face, eyeing each arm of the pincer.

The pincers were certainly large enough to grab a person. Elena patted his arm, trying to reassure Gilbert that everything was going to be okay.

Just then, at the bottom of the craft, a large hatch, nearly as wide as the train car, cracked open. The edge of the hatch lowered on two massive pistons, forming a ramp. Steam hissed in trailing plumes from valves in the piston pipes as the edge of the hatch paused just inches above the roof of the train. A man in a white sea captain's uniform stood at the top of the ramp. He had a broad grey beard and a bushy moustache to match. His moustache blended with his beard so well that the only indication that he had a mouth at all was the stubby, plain, black smoking pipe that protruded from the hairy mass.

'Don't mind the oculavermi. Just had to make sure we were positioned right and weren't knocking anyone off. Safety first, right?' the captain shouted down. 'Well, don't just stand there staring. Come aboard! We've got a schedule to keep.'

He motioned for them to step forward with a dramatic sweep of his arm – smoke snorting out from his nose.

Jerome was first to stride up the ramp, his cane tapping a couple of times as he went.

'Peter, there's something…' Jerome started to say upon reaching the captain.

'Coming from the south,' the captain interrupted. 'Yes, we saw it just as we turned to make our approach. I expect it's Ulysses Rack,' he added, taking his pipe in hand as he puffed out a cloud of smoke.

Elena arrived at the top of the ramp next.

'And who is this fetching creature?' the captain leered.

Gilbert came stumbling up behind her, not having heard the captain's remark.

'The name's Gilbert, Gilbert Penn, frontier journalist.' Gilbert thrust out his hand. It drew smiles and chuckles from

Jerome, Elena, and the captain.

'Well met, Mr Penn. I'm pretty sure we'll give you plenty to write about.'

The captain laughed as he made a gesture with his left hand to some unseen individual in the hull's dim lamp-lit darkness. The ramp began to close as the ship arced northeast, away from the train.

'Lady Elena Saphuthest, I introduce to you Peter Mennis. Captain of this amazing flying contraption and leader of the Sonora Aero Club.'

Jerome made grand sweeping gestures to each of them, fitting of their titles. Elena gave a polite, silent nod to the captain.

'The Sonora, what now?'

Gilbert fumbled around with one hand in the knapsack he had slung across his chest while his other hand reached for the pen in the breast pocket of his baggy brown waistcoat.

'Plenty of time for that later, young man,' Captain Mennis said, taking Gilbert firmly by the shoulder. 'We really need to head topside and see exactly what we have intercepting us. Please, follow me.'

The journey to the uppermost, or "poop", deck of the vessel was a labyrinth of dimly lit wooden corridors and stairs. There were five levels altogether, not counting the poop deck. The lowest three levels were reserved for cargo and crew quarters, while the following two floors above were noisy, rumbling steam-filled layers. These upper two floors had very few areas with a ceiling or floor to separate the two. Metal gangways formed something of a labyrinth, twisting up, down and around past giant gears, cogs, pipes, and axles, like a tangled mass of metal snakes. Valves hissed, massive click hammers banged, flywheels whirred, and enormous tension springs moaned as the group made their way through the middle of the ship.

Goggled crewmen in long, heavy leather coats could be seen everywhere, frantically flipping switches, cranking levers, hammering this and welding that. Gilbert couldn't even comprehend what some of the tasks were. One man, for example, was pouring some sort of thick orange liquid into what looked like a revolving meat grinder, while another hulk of a man worked a massive rotating lever as though he were rowing an enormous oar. The purpose of either of these tasks was utterly elusive.

This middle area was also illuminated much better than the rest of the lower decks. The light source was a huge, oval, clear glass vat filled with a roiling blue, glowing gas.

'What is that?' Gilbert asked loudly, pointing as though the others might not have noticed the vast, radiant blue ovoid.

'That, my boy, is the very heart of this ship. Full of NB gas, as the inventor, your friend here, calls it.' The captain pointed a thumb at Jerome. 'We heat it and pressurise it into a plasma. Not an easy task but, without it, we'd have a much harder time keeping this big gal moving through the air the way she does. Which reminds me, Jerome, one of the fellas back in Sonora, that German fella, Wolfgang, says he's going to need another shipment of the NB powder.'

'That shouldn't be a problem. I'll let Ivan in San Francisco know to expect him. Payment in the usual manner?'

'Of course, of course.' Mennis waved a hand dismissively, smoke puffing out with every word. 'Don't know what a man would want with all of that ash.'

As they emerged topside, Gilbert blinked, trying to adjust

his eyes to the glaring sun. Though they were still in shadow, the relative brightness was still blinding. The deck was as much a spectacle as the level below. They were near the ship's bow, though it was hard to tell which end was forward and which was stern. Both ends of the vessel were mirrors of one another in shape and function. Large, bladed rudders made of wood and metal were at both ends, shaped like giant axe heads. The tops of these blades towered twenty feet above the deck.

Before his eyes had adjusted, Gilbert thought the group emerged next to a large mast, but this ship had no sails. The large paddle wheels on either side midship provided locomotion. It was something else entirely casting the shadow that they were standing in. He looked up to find that the mast-like metal post was topped, maybe thirty feet high, with a large brass ball. The brass ball was forty feet in diameter with a ring of twenty-foot-tall rectangular posts whirling around it. Perplexingly, they didn't appear to be attached to the ball in any way, and he had no way of telling exactly how many posts were rotating around the ball; they were moving far too fast. An identical structure was at the other end of the ship.

'Let me guess,' he said, pointing up at the metal ball as he looked to Jerome. 'Rewarium.'

Jerome just winked and smiled broadly.

The captain took a few steps ahead of the group, spread his arms wide, and puffed out his chest. 'Lady and gents, welcome aboard the Maeldun.'

Elena gave another silent, polite bow. Gilbert was scribbling away in his notebook.

'Always a wonder, and an honour, Pete,' Jerome said brightly. 'Thanks for helping us out with this little quest of ours.'

'Always in for one of your adventures, my boy, especially this close to home.' The captain pointed his pipe at Jerome for emphasis. 'Now, if you'll all join me on the bridge, we'll see if we can get a better look at that crow's tail out there.'

'Crow's tail?' Gilbert questioned, looking up from his notebook.

'The vessel that may be following us,' Elena said in a low tone.

Gilbert nodded, writing the term and definition down.

The bridge of the vessel topped a four-story wooden tower located midship, the ship's castle. It was a curious structure. It had curved walls facing fore and aft that tapered to points to the left and right, forming arches that one would have to pass through to access either end of the vessel. Intricate carvings of four intertwined serpents, two wrapped around each other on either side of the tower, decorated the tapered edges. The serpents' bodies curved over the arches and up to the top-most level of the castle. Atop the heads of these serpents, on either side of the tower, were two enormous carvings of winged horses. Only the fore half of their bodies were visible, their hoofs posed as if frozen mid-flail as they reared up. Though the depictions of the creatures were far more realistic, the stacked carvings reminded Gilbert of the totem poles he had seen in his travels. Nestled in the horses' widespread wings, and rising another twenty feet above the bridge, were two large, red stacks that constantly billowed the stream of clouds that Gilbert had noted earlier. A lattice of artfully twisted, wrought iron rods served as support, filling the significant gaps between each floor.

On the far side of the structure from where the group had emerged onto the deck, there was an elevator cage. The four of them crowded into the tiny metal chamber of the elevator. A crew member, clad in a long white coat, slid the collapsible cage door closed and heaved the large lever, sending them slowly up the tower to the bridge.

It was a bright room with large windows all around. Four crew members here, dressed in white linen, vested suits with short coats and wide dark blue ties, were busy at the controls of different panels that ringed the room. Each of these panels was full of dials, levers, switches, gauges, and tiny, blinking electrical lights. One of the bridge's crew glanced up as the elevator arrived. He was positioned at a large central island panel and had been busy watching over a wood-framed paper topographical map that was slowly scrolling across the tabletop.

'Captain on the bridge,' he announced loudly, snapping to attention and thumping his right fist to his chest in salute.

The other three quickly followed his example.

'As you were,' the captain puffed, waving a hand as if he found the formality just a little annoying. 'What do we have, Mr Wicker?'

'A dreadnaught, Sir. Dirigible headed straight our way. Still too far out to make her markings, and she's not responding to our hail flashes and...'

'Yes? Out with it, son.'

'She's closing, Sir.'

The crewman glanced down, trying to avoid the captain's judging eyes.

'Closing?' Captain Mennis sounded more appalled than surprised.

Gilbert was frantically chronicling everything he could in his notebook.

'Yes, Sir. She's fast for a dirigible. It has to be the Cetus,' the crewman said, looking back up at the captain, 'but according to the range clock, we should have a four-hour lead on her.'

'If it is Ulysses, I'm not worried about that flying, steel cow of his catching us. He'll be dealing with that beam wind. It's those damned gnats of his. He'll be launching those damnable things the moment he has the range. Let me know if he squeezes out any more speed from that balloon, and have the gunners prep their stations and stand ready. We probably have about an hour, and it's going to get ugly.'

'We should nearly be at our destination in an hour, no?' Jerome sounded a little concerned.

It was the first time, in the two weeks that Gilbert had been travelling with the man, that Jerome had expressed anything but arrogant confidence.

'Gnats?' Gilbert tossed in. 'And how does this thing even fly?'

'Yes, shouldn't be a worry,' the captain replied to Jerome in a reassuring tone. 'and you'll see the gnats soon enough, boy,' he said, turning back to Gilbert. 'You're in for quite a show.'

'We mustn't fail. Not this close,' Elena said in a stern whisper to Jerome, grabbing him softly by the elbow.

The captain overheard her comment. 'Don't you fret none, Miss. I've crossed swords with Ulysses Rack and his thugs before. I'm surprised he's come back for more. You must have really annoyed the man this time, Jerome.'

'I may have misappropriated one of his misappropriated shipments a month or so back,' Jerome said with a sly smile, leaning into his cane.

'I'm sure,' the captain snickered contemplatively, letting out another fog of smoke.

'His spies, as you know, are everywhere.' Jerome pulled a gold watch from his vest pocket, popping it open. 'Clearly, word got to him of what we seek in the canyon. An hour, you say. Time enough for tea then.'

The captain grumbled something a little incoherently, readjusted his pipe and waved to another crewman, a gauntly thin, stern-looking woman with dirty blonde hair.

'See these three to the guest quarters. Then head down to the boiler and have a talk with the black coats. See if we can't get our wheels eating more sky.'

'Aye, Captain,' the woman gave a sharp salute, fist-to-chest. 'Follow me, please,' she said gruffly, walking past the ship's three guests and entering the elevator.

They followed.

The guest quarters' common room was decorated in luxurious style, with all the comfort and design one would expect from the sitting room of a stately mansion. Dark velvet red drapes ridiculously over-framed small porthole windows on either end of the room. Six flickering lamps, held aloft by sconces designed in a vine motif, provided most of the light in the room. A thick tapestry rug from India covered most of the polished wood floor. The trophy head of a gazelle and a glinting blue and silver swordfish adorned the walls, speaking to the breadth of the Maeldun's travels. All that was missing, Gilbert thought, was an immense stone fireplace.

Gilbert spent the next hour in this warmly decorated common room, nestled deep in a plush red velvet smoking chair, tossing question after question at Jerome. The first two being where they were headed and who Ulysses Rack was. Jerome was candid with the journalist. Gilbert couldn't be expected to properly chronicle Jerome's travels if he was keeping every little thing about the trip a secret. Besides, he and the mysteriously veiled Lady Saphuthest were holding a big enough secret about themselves to make up for any other information he might divulge.

He explained they were heading to the Grand Canyon, where they sought a hidden cave entrance leading to what some called Cibola or El Dorado, the empire of gold.

Ulysses Rack and his crew were veterans of the great Portuguese Air War of 1890 that had seen Florida become a Portuguese territory. In the last days of the war, Ulysses and his dreadnaught-class dirigible, the Cetus, were holding the line assured that reinforcements were coming. In a gambit to take control of Mexico, the Reformed Southern Coalition abandoned what they felt to be the worthless swamps of Florida. The reinforcements that Ulysses was expecting never came, and he found himself forced to flee against the Portuguese fleet. However, the Coalition's strategy had taken the Portuguese by surprise, and the loss of the Mexican territories forced them to negotiate an end to the war. Ulysses and his men, rightfully feeling betrayed by the Coalition, struck out on their own. They quickly became the most notorious group of pirates, smugglers, and treasure seekers, not only in the Americas but around the world.

Jerome's own penchant for seeking out lost mysteries and ancient treasures had found him crossing paths with Ulysses and his men on several occasions. The encounters were always messy affairs, and, so far, Jerome had always managed to stay a step ahead of the hot-headed pirate captain. Truthfully, he had come to enjoy thwarting Captain Rack's activities and had taken to going out of his way to annoy the man.

This particular situation, however, had found its way to Jerome, or rather, Lady Saphuthest had. A week before running into Gilbert, Jerome had received a trans-Pacific pneumatic letter from Lady Saphuthest, an old friend from his days in Morocco, explaining that she needed his assistance. It had come to her attention that Ulysses was seeking out El Dorado and that he was getting close to finding it. Knowing Jerome took great pleasure in interfering with the pirate's exploits, she assured Jerome that she knew exactly where to find the fabled city, but they would need to hurry if they were to beat Captain Rack to its discovery. Jerome suspected there was something more to the Lady's interest in finding El Dorado in such a rush. Still, she had been right in assuming he wouldn't be able to resist another opportunity to vex the pirate captain.

'But no one really knows where El Dorado is, or if it's even real,' Gilbert complained. 'And isn't it supposed to be somewhere in South America? I mean, the Spanish and the Mayans and all that? Right?'

'Well, if that is the Cetus coming from the south, clearly that's where he was looking too,' Jerome said, taking a sip of tea that the ship's cook had been kind enough to send up to their quarters. 'Say, Gil, old man, you haven't seen my night vision goggles, have you?'

'I expect that they're with the rest of our luggage,' Gilbert responded, looking a little exasperated.

'Yes?' Jerome looked up from his tea.

'On the train,' Gilbert grumbled.

'Quite right,' Jerome nodded, raising his cup in a toast to Gilbert's astuteness. 'Hadn't truly thought that one through. We should look into hiring a manservant, someone who can keep track of such things. You know, I once met a British professor while travelling through Africa who had an orangutan as his butler. Charming fellow... the orangutan. The professor was a bit chatty.'

Gilbert ignored the comments, continuing with his barrage of questions. Most of these were now aimed at Lady Elena; questions like who she was exactly or how she and Jerome met, what the urgency in reaching El Dorado was, or why she constantly kept her face covered. Elena dodged all of his queries and, in her subtle, silky-voiced, flirtatious way, navigated the conversation back on Gilbert. Before long, she had him divulging much of his dramatically dull life story before becoming a frontier journalist. As if rapt by every detail, Elena had slinked seductively across the room, her gaze locked upon the awkward little reporter, and sat herself down upon the arm of his chair. By the end of Gilbert's blushing, stammering ramble, she had slid herself onto his lap. She adjusted his thin black bow tie and tapped him playfully on the nose as she popped back to her feet.

'Oh, he's a darling one, Jerome. I think he might be the last sincere man in the world. You'll have to keep him,' she chuckled in a soft, sultry voice.

There was something odd about her voice, Gilbert thought, as he continued to blush in silence. Not only was it perfectly feminine in tone, not shrill or nasal in any sort of way, but it was just generally perfect. Every word she spoke, whether aloud or a whisper, was unerringly annunciated. It was both mesmerising and unnerving.

'Vacuum bladders with magnetically spun NB plasma casings,' Jerome said flatly in a complete non sequitur that snapped Gilbert from his stupor.

'What now?' Gilbert shook his head, wondering if he had missed something.

'How this thing – this ship – flies. You had asked the captain earlier. Thought you might want to scribble that down in your book.'

Jerome pulled out his pocket watch as he spoke to check the time. Just then, a loud bell began ringing.

'Given that an hour has passed, I expect that is not a good thing,' he said, simultaneously slipping the watch back in its pocket and placing his teacup down on the long, low table in the centre of the room.

Two more bells started ringing somewhere much further away within the Maeldun. Then came shouts; orders being relayed throughout the ship.

The deep pounding, firing chatter of the Maeldun's enormous Gatling guns rumbled loudly below the trio.

'Yes, that's most definitely bad.'

Jerome shot a concerned look toward Elena.

As one would find on a phonograph, a copper horn sticking out of the wall by the entryway suddenly blared out the voice of the captain.

'You lot stay inside and stay low; low as you can. We've got incoming screamers.'

'What? What are screamers?' Gilbert asked, confused as to what was happening.

As if to answer the question, an awful sound came then, growing louder by the second. It was a hideous combination of a large growling dog and the screeching of metal grinding on metal. The sound not only grew louder but multiplied and soon became deafening. Adding to the cacophony came a violent whooshing sound, followed by another and another. Fast-moving shadows strobed the light streaming through the four small round windows in the room. The whole room shook then. Gilbert thought that the small windows would shatter; they rattled so violently. He went to peek out of one of the windows to catch a glimpse of what was causing such a disturbance, but Jerome could already see from his vantage point, and lunged at Gilbert.

'No! Get down!'

He knocked Gilbert to the floor, thrusting his right arm in front of them both as he tapped a spot on the left side of his hat brim. A metal shield spiralled out from a bracelet on his right wrist like an expanding iris. From beneath the front brim of Jerome's hat, in the blink of an eye, six metal slats dropped in quick succession, snapping themselves into a single, rigid sheet that completely covered his face. A single, slim, dark glass slit provided sight through the square protective mask. Both shields were made of Jerome's rewarium.

A flurry of metal projectiles ripped through the cabin, then a dozen or more ricocheted off of Jerome's well-timed protective coverings. Streams of light shone like white laser beams through the spray of holes. Jerome swung around to see if Elena was all right.

She was standing calmly, precisely where she had been the moment before, completely unharmed. Elena strode over to where Jerome had been sitting with his tea earlier and calmly picked up his cane.

'You'll be needing this, yes?'

Jerome threw a glance at Gilbert. He was a little ruffled from being knocked to the floor, but was otherwise unharmed. Jerome darted over to Elena, giving her a quick tip of his hat in gratitude as he grabbed the cane from her hand. Brandishing it like the rifle it was, he dashed out the door.

Outside, it was chaos. Crew members were running in every direction. Others, armed with long, magnetic rail guns, were scanning the sky frantically. Streams of black smoke surrounded the ship. The rumbling sound of multiple, large Gatling guns thundered up from the deck below. Out across the deck, Jerome could see the single pilot flying machines, the screamers, arcing around the ship to make another strafing approach. As he watched, one exploded in a burst of flames and black smoke, clearly caught in the return fire of the Maeldun's guns. It left what looked a little like the silhouette of a palm tree made of smoke floating in the air.

Screamers were unique to the dreadnaught class of warship, which typically carried twenty on a platform mounted on top of the dirigible. They could travel much faster than the warships, but had a limited supply of fuel. The best pilots could make four strafing runs before needing to make the return journey to their warship for refuelling. Inexperienced pilots running out of fuel counted for as many crashed screamers as those shot down by enemy fire. They were hard to hit as fast as they were. Novices were not piloting the screamers attacking now. Just to fly the contraption required a high level of skill, but these were some of the best screamer aces of the air war.

Screamers were nothing much more than a large turbine mounted between a dual-layer of swept-back wings, the bottom wings being broader and longer than the top. Machine guns were mounted on either side between the top and bottom wings and could be fired separately. Stabilising, vertical tail fins in the back formed what looked like a tiny fishtail. There was little more to their design. They were small, the reason Captain Mennis referred to them as gnats. Without room for a cockpit, the pilots were exposed, straddled on top. Their legs looped into straps, pedals at their feet, controlled speed and yaw, while handlebars provided pitch, roll, and weapon firing.

Jerome spun around, trying to gauge the number of pilots attacking the Maeldun. He guessed at ten, but there were almost certainly more out of view below the ship. He ran to the edge of the deck, hoping to single out one of the screamers.

As Jerome looked over the edge, he spotted three screamers. Two of them suddenly burst into orange fireballs, victims of the Maeldun's constant gunfire. The wreckage and the bodies of the pilots rained down on the landscape far below. Jerome kept his eyes on the third as it made a wide sloping arc toward the rear of the Maeldun. He took his shot. His cane made a loud, angry buzzing sound as a vibrant green beam of plasma streaked from its barrel. *They are so fast*, he thought; it was a mix of admiration and frustration. His aim had fallen well behind his target. He would need to lead his shots far more than he anticipated. Suddenly, the deck was exploding in small bursts of wood all around him. The rapid-fire of a strafing screamer's bullets were tearing up the deck. Bullets sparked off of Jerome's arm shield as he watched a crewman take several screamer bullets and fall over the side of the ship. The screamer roared just feet above Jerome's head, blanketing the deck in its black exhaust. The smoke was chokingly dense, making it hard to breathe, and more disturbingly, hard to see. It dissipated quickly in the wind, but it had been enough to be disoriented and enough to let the screamer dive away below the ship out Jerome's line of sight.

Another screamer caught Jerome's eye. It was coming in low, at an angle from behind the Maeldun. It looked like an attempt to take out the guns, or perhaps the paddlewheel on the starboard side. Jerome quickly took a shot. There was no time to line up the target. The plasma beam shot a little wide, shearing off the end of the screamers top left wing. It sent the screamer into a diving spin and was soon out of view.

A loud explosion from the other side rocked the ship violently, sending Jerome over the edge of the deck. He was barely able to throw a hand out in time to hang on to the ship's railing. Grey smoke streamed from the port side of the Maeldun. The wheel on that side came to a gear-grinding halt as the airship heaved hard, leaning in that direction. The sudden motion flipped Jerome back on to the steeply sloping deck. He tumbled uncontrollably for several feet.

Two more screamers streaked overhead on a perpendicular trajectory, riddling the bridge with a rain of bullets.

'Pete!' Jerome shouted.

It had been the final assault run; the screamers were turning back to the Cetus.

Jerome flicked the switches, quickly retracted his arm and face shields, and stumbled his way across the crooked deck back to the ship's castle. The crewman who operated the elevator was nowhere to be seen, and Jerome wasn't sure he would trust the elevator to function safely at the moment. He scrambled up a nearby spiralling wrought iron staircase, stopping briefly on the second floor to see that Elena and Gilbert were okay.

Gilbert looked terribly rattled, but they were unharmed. Jerome continued up to the bridge.

The scene on the bridge was less than encouraging. Splinters of wood and glass were everywhere; all the crew were bloody messes slumped over each of their station panels.

Captain Mennis was face down, unmoving, on the map table. A continuous red streak was slowly being pulled out from his profusely bleeding head as the map continued to scroll across the table, tracking the ship's position above the land.

'Pete!'

Jerome rushed over to the captain, who was still clutching his pipe in his bloody right hand. He righted the old airman, propping him up, seated on the floor against the bridge's nearby back wall. The captain's face was streaked with lacerations and blood. His eyes fluttered open weakly, not quite able to focus on Jerome.

'Keep her in the air, Jerome,' the barely conscious captain muttered. He coughed up blood and tried again, a little louder this time. 'Keep her...' his voice trailed off as he let out his last breath.

Jerome was at a loss, hardly believing that his old friend could be gone.

A groan came from a far corner of the bridge below one of the control panels. It was the hard-looking female crewman. She was cut and bruised, but looked unharmed. Jerome rushed over to her, helping her to her feet.

'Are you okay? What is your name?'

'Harriet. Third Mate, Harriet Stocks.' She was wide-eyed but trying to hold her composure.

'I think you may be the captain now,' Jerome said sullenly.

'Will you be able to fly her on your own?'

'I'll need some help,' she answered hesitantly, 'but I'm pretty sure I just heard the captain tell you to keep her. I'd say that makes you the captain, Sir.'

Jerome just looked at her in stunned silence, vaguely pointing toward the still form of Captain Mennis, trying to find the proper words through his emotion to correct her.

She straightened herself into a stance of professional command, gathering her wits and brushing off her uniform.

'He would have wanted it this way,' she added, eyeing Jerome. The stoic look upon her face indicated that she would not be argued with. 'Sir. In any case, we arrived at the coordinates of your destination just as the Cetus attacked. You'll just need to let me know where you want to throw anchor and mooring lines. I'm assuming you intended on disembarking.'

'Uh, yes. Yes. I'll need to fetch Lady Saphuthest,' Jerome said, still staring at his departed friend. 'Never anyone as punctual as ol' Peter,' he whispered to himself with a sigh.

'We'll have an hour or two to assess our losses and make what repairs we can before the Cetus arrives,' Harriet said, moving to one of the panels, flipping several switches and a large lever. The Maeldun shuddered in immediate response. 'What I know is the attack took out one wheel, a few of our port side guns and the midship flight bladder. We'll be listing starboard for a while, and our manoeuvrability will be limited. It will not be a quick fix.'

'Yes, good,' Jerome said, his mind streaming through too many thoughts at once. 'I mean, awful, uh, rather, you seem to have it well enough in hand.'

'Hardly, Sir, but we'll do. I don't expect a second wave of

screamers. They didn't want us down, just limping, and they certainly accomplished that. Whatever you're here for, I suggest you hurry. We should try to crawl away while we can.'

She thumped a fist to her chest.

'Right, when I get back, we're going to have to work on that,' he said, wincing at her salute.

He hesitatingly brought a fist slowly up to his chest in return. He headed down the stairs to the guest quarters.

Elena was impressed. The crew of the Maeldun had navigated to the location she had communicated, through Jerome, precisely. They were five hundred feet above the river on the canyon floor. Within the canyon wall, shielded from view both above and below by jutting rock, was a cave opening approximately twenty feet in diameter. The Maeldun was hovering just yards away from it, the entrance to what some called El Dorado or Cibola. To her, and in fact, its actual name was Kan Vilhuda.

Harriet had done a fantastic job rallying the crew. The injured were being tended to. Repairs that could be made were well underway, and with a few well-placed grapple-tipped mooring lines, she was able to kedge the ship right next to the cave. The crew had aligned the Maeldun's deck, almost perfectly, with the bottom ledge of the cave. A gangplank was put in place to bridge the gap.

'Will you need a security detail?' Harriet asked Jerome as he, Elena, and Gilbert set to make their way across to the cave.

'No, I think we'll be fine. The Lady knows her way around.'

'Very well, Sir. Be safe, be swift. We'll need to leave in sixty-three minutes if we're to stay ahead of the Cetus,' Harriet said flatly as another crewman came by with a log for her to sign.

A distant black trail of smoke over Harriet's left shoulder caught Jerome's eye then.

'Looks like we have someone who forgot to go home.'

It was a single screamer, flying erratically. He couldn't be sure, but it may have been the screamer whose wing he had clipped during the attack.

'Make sure that would-be hero goes out in a blaze of glory if you catch my meaning,' he said, pointing at the distant screamer.

Harriet looked over her shoulder, looking immediately distressed.

'You have got this,' Jerome said, firmly grabbing her by both shoulders. She was equal to his six-foot stature, maybe even an inch taller. He looked her square in the eyes. 'You have got this, and you must leave without us if we're not back in time.' He shot her a wide smile, tipping his hat to her as he turned to cross the gangway. Elena and Gilbert were already across. 'You certainly can't be any worse than her current captain,' he added.

He didn't notice Harriet almost cracking a smile as he turned to the cave.

'Hold this for me, will you?' Elena said to Gilbert as they walked into the cave. It was one of her long purple gloves.

He glanced at her bare arm. It was not the gears, rods, and wires sort of prosthetic that he was expecting. Her arm was reflectively radiant in the shadowed light of the cave entrance. It was a smooth, metallic gold with finely etched lines that glinted white as they caught the faint light. From what Gilbert could tell, the lines accommodated her arms' mobility, segmenting her outer skin, expanding to hint at more of the same golden surface below whenever she moved. He was fascinated.

'Thank you,' she said politely and then, pointing her golden arm into the darkness of the cave, her fingertips erupted with a brilliant white-blue light.

It was illuminating their way as clearly as though daylight was filling the corridor.

It was evident that the cave was not naturally formed. The walls were too straight and met at right angles, with the floor and ceiling. Chisel marks could be seen everywhere. Just fifty feet in, the cave floor was covered in smooth stone tile. The walls were covered with brightly painted, carved hieroglyphics.

'I wonder what they say?' Gilbert marvelled. 'They almost look Egyptian.'

Jerome chuckled at this.

'They are, of a sort,' Lady Elena said. Gilbert could hear the smile in her voice, even if he couldn't see it through the veils. 'It is a record of the journey made by seven royal families and their followers that came here to establish a better world. An empire based on peace, harmony, art, music, and literature. They gave up their own kingdoms to follow one foolish dreamer.'

One hundred feet in, the tunnel ended, intersected by another, grander hall. Its ceiling stretched fifty feet high in magnificent pointed arches. An immense figure, carved in one solid piece of white marble, sat cross-legged before them. Its hands cupped a bowl in its lap. The figure's hair, or perhaps it was some manner of a helmet, was made up of thousands of tiny spheres set in tightly clustered rows, culminating in a ball atop its head.

'Who is that?' Gilbert pondered aloud. 'It almost looks like a depiction of Buddha, but it's, well…' he stammered and blushed, resorting to simply pointing at first. 'It's a woman!' he got out finally, still pointing at the statue's ample, bare breasts.

'It's me,' Elena said quietly.

With her gloved hand, she pulled off her hat and veils. She was staggeringly beautiful. Her face had a mesmerising symmetry, made of the same hard gold as her arm. Her eyes were large, almost unnaturally so, and perfectly almond-shaped. The irises of her eyes were so black there was no hint of her pupils. Although she had no eyelashes, her eyes had the illusion of such. They were lined with a series of elegantly curving black bands that flared out onto her temples. These same black bands formed eyebrows of a sort as well, curling elegantly like vines onto the side of her head. Her voluptuous lips were a deep, dark red, seemingly just as hard and metallic as the rest of her. Curiously though, as she spoke, it was evident that her lips were pliant, moving as smoothly and with all the expression of human lips.

'They followed me here, ten thousand years ago.'

'What?' Gilbert exclaimed. 'What are you? Ten thousand years? How is that even possible?' He turned to Jerome. 'Did you know this? Do you believe any of this?'

'I know much of it and know it to be true,' Jerome said, clearing his voice and pushing back his hat as he craned his neck, continuing to examine the grandly tall bare-breasted statue. 'And you have to admit, she looks amazing for her age. It hardly looks like she's aged a day in ten thousand years.'

Elena shot Jerome a slightly disapproving glance.

'Perhaps we'll divulge some of your secrets next, old man.'

At that moment, from the other end of the cave came the distinctive rattling thunder of the Maeldun's guns, followed by the horrible sound of a quickly approaching screamer. The trio looked back in the direction of all the noise. From their location, the cave opening was just a white dot of light. It suddenly darkened, and the cave filled with the deafening sound of the rogue screamer.

'Run!' shouted Jerome.

'This way!' Elena cried back, taking Gilbert by the arm, pulling him quickly down the left corridor.

Jerome followed close on their heels.

There was a horrendous sound of scraping of metal on stone followed by the teeth grinding crash of buckling metal. Gilbert looked back, but the corridor behind them was washed in darkness. Only small orange flames could be seen flickering where the three of them had been standing before the statue only moments ago.

Elena led them down the corridor, turning right between two cat-headed statues that bore crossed palm fronds that formed an arch.

'Stop!' she said, holding her arms out to block the way of her two companions.

The light from her fingers had not diminished, but here, suddenly, they illuminated nothing. A deep void of endless black was before them.

'Stop!' came her voice again, echoing somewhere distant in the darkness.

'Exactly the sort of moment my night vision goggles would have come in handy,' Jerome quipped.

'Feh Alnwar Jakar!' Elena commanded.

Her voice boomed at an inhuman volume, reverberating in the deep black distance, echoing seven times. In the darkness ahead, a small blue flame appeared, and then another, and another. Soon hundreds of the luminous blue tongues of fire flickered distantly, their light teased at surrounding structures and shapes. A clap of thunder followed, and the trio was bathed in a brilliant yellow-white light. This new light illuminated the vast cavern before them, and the view was dizzying.

They could see then that they stood at the top of a grand staircase that descended at least a hundred and eighty feet. The height of the cave's ceiling was more difficult to discern. Hundreds of feet up was a swirling, dazzlingly luminous yellow mass. Below stretched a vast city made of pink granite, white marble, and lustrous gold. It extended as far into the distance as the eye could see.

Narrow, bricked streets snaked between thinly separated buildings of grand architectural design, winding up, down and around seven discernible levels. Tall, ornate flying buttresses of stone supported many of the buildings and roadways on these lofty levels, giving much of the city the feel of being one enormous gothic cathedral. There were grand archways with Grecian columns topped by intricately carved triangular or rectangular capstones. Pyramids of both Egyptian and Mayan design dotted the city, as well as several enormous ziggurats. Cone-shaped buildings surrounded many pyramids arranged in a fractal pattern of small, identical cones that twisted around the pyramids' exteriors. Other buildings were adorned with a multitude of highly detailed carvings, while others had colossal figures either atop or before their entrances. There were depictions of gryphons, men, women, sphinx-like jackals, and winged beings that, to Gilbert, looked like angels.

Amongst all of this, there was one building that stood out. It was a perfect gold sphere at the end of a long, gently sloping bridge of bright white stone. The bridge was impossibly suspended. It had no arches or columns below to support it, but passed through five floating, flat stone rings. Each ring, fifty feet in diameter, embossed with mysterious symbols plated in gold, rotated slowly clockwise. They were as just as impossibly suspended in the air as the walkway that passed through them.

'That is where we must go,' she said to Gilbert with a smile as she noticed his gaze in that direction.

'What – what is up there, exactly?' Jerome asked, pointing his cane to the ceiling.

'Another time, Jerome. I promise,' Elena said, making her way down the steps.

Gilbert followed, his nose in his notebook, writing as much detail as possible, and making very rough, quick sketches of some of the structures.

'I need to invest in a camera,' he grumbled. 'No one is going to believe any of this.'

He looked up momentarily as he stumbled a bit on the steps, noting it would be quite a fall if he were not more careful.

They made their way down several streets, their feet echoed with every step. The city's emptiness was eerie, and it made many of the statues, although beautiful, somehow sinister, as they loomed overhead. They looked down upon the three of them with unblinking eyes.

'What happened here?' Gilbert asked as they arrived at the base of the floating bridge. 'Where did everyone go?'

'Maybe they heard that there's gold in the Yukon,' Jerome said sarcastically. 'That's been known to clear out a town or two.'

Elena shot Jerome an admonishing look, deeming his remark as inappropriate.

'This city thrived for thousands of years. In time, as our

population grew and the attitudes and values of the young no longer aligned with the old ways, as always happens, some ventured out into the surrounding lands establishing new cities, new empires in the sun. They would always come back to us for trade, for knowledge, or to arbitrate peace in their disputes. The wisdom of those who lived here continued to be revered, and this place was considered sacred. None would dare a conflict with us for fear of condemning their souls and dishonouring their families for generations.

In the year 1005, a woman and her husband, having travelled from distant lands in the north, came seeking my people's council. They told a story of pale-skinned men with hairy faces, savage barbarians who came from the great sea as we once had, who had attacked their city without provocation. They wanted us to provide them with protective technology or perhaps transmit a message of distress on their behalf to the other cities of the south. They hoped our involvement might persuade the others to set aside their rivalries, to fend off these strange men from the sea who would surely prove to be a threat to them all.

In the end, it did not matter. For these two from the north had brought with them a great plague. It ravaged the people of this city entirely and destroyed all but small pockets of people throughout the continent. Empires crumbled; once-great cities, now empty, were swallowed up by the wilderness. After a few hundred years, this city faded to all but a near-forgotten legend, and the grandeur of this land and its people became myths; garbled folklore of gods and spirits told around fires by the nomadic descendants of the few who survived the plague.'

'I'll make a note to erect a plaque at the door,' came a gruff voice some distance behind the trio. 'The tourists really go for that sort of crap.'

It was Ulysses Rack. He was an intimidating looking, large, stalky man, not quite muscular, but certainly not fat. His jaw was thick and wide; the sort lesser men would break their fists on. It was peppered with a permanent stubble of black and grey. His hair was thick and black as coal, like a man half of his 45 years, but his wide grey sideburns hinted at his actual age. He wore a black-coloured bastardisation of the grey Coalition military garb. His wide-legged, thick cotton trousers had two red stripes running down each leg rather than yellow. Instead of a short grey jacket, he wore a long black leather coat with wide lapels and a stiff, high collar. Four red stripes adorned his epaulettes and extra-wide cuffs.

'Do those things see in the dark? They do, don't they?' Jerome shouted back at the man.

He was referring to the glowing red goggles covering Rack's eyes. They did, in fact, grant the captain some degree of night vision, but he ignored Jerome's question.

'No sudden moves, Saint-Earl,' the captain growled back. He was brandishing a large arc pistol in his left hand, aimed directly at Jerome. It was a complicated-looking piece of weaponry, resembling a flintlock pistol with three barrels, each wrapped in loosely wound copper coils. Three-inch spikes protruded from each of the outer two barrels. Two small amber tubes on the left side crackled with sparks of electricity. 'That infernal cane of yours did enough damage to my screamer. I'd rather not have it ruin my coat as well.'

'That was you!' Jerome laughed. 'Had I known, I would have aimed a little more carefully. And honestly, what captain rides out on a screamer himself? So hands-on, so virile.'

Jerome raised a fist in the air, snarling out the latter, mimicking Rack's rasping voice with great exaggeration.

'Shut your mouth, ya gah-dammed dandy smart arse,' the captain barked back.

He began walking toward the three. A hollow-sounding voice emitted from his hip then.

'The bats are fed, Captain. Should we launch again and finish her off?'

Rack grabbed the wooden box at his hip. Alternating red and green lights blinked above a series of drilled holes on its face. Two thick wire antennae protruded from the top in a vee shape, arcing back together and wrapping around one another to form a hoop. He flipped one of two metal switches on the side with his thumb. The green light stayed on as he spoke into the box.

'Negative. We'll need her to haul the gold, and I'm in the mood to double the size of our fleet.'

He flipped the switch again; the green light went out, and the red light came on.

'Aye, Captain. ETA two hours, five minutes. Out,' the voice came back.

The red and green lights began alternating again. He returned the box to the leather holster on his belt.

'Now, which of you is going to jump first?' Ulysses said with as light a tone as his gravelly voice could muster. 'What? You didn't think I had any plan of sparing the lot of you? I only followed you long enough to figure out where the truly great treasure is. Clearly, that is this big ball here. So over you go. Let's start with the little fella, what d'ya say?'

There was nowhere for them to go. They were trapped on

the bridge. A river of mercury flowed below. A drop from this height onto the mercury would be fatal; it might as well be a solid river of granite. They could run to the spherical building just a few yards ahead but be trapped, or they could try to charge the captain, but that didn't seem like a sensible option.

Naturally, this is the option Jerome chose. He lunged, dodging slightly to the left, then to the right. He was surprisingly fast. Ulysses fired his shock pistol. A great arc of electricity burst from the gun with a loud crack. It narrowly missed Jerome, pulverising a small section of the walkway's marble railing. Jerome raised his cane and fired, but Ulysses had anticipated the move and managed to side-step the wide green plasma beam. He rushed forward, knocking Jerome's cane from his hands, sending the weapon spinning across the walkway, and grabbed Jerome by the neck.

'Run!' Elena urged Gilbert. 'He will not be a match for me.' Her tone was ominous.

Gilbert stumbled backwards, losing his balance as he tried to turn.

'You're sure we can't talk this out?' Jerome joked, barely getting the words out through Ulysses' grip.

The captain just sneered. He had Jerome well off the ground as he thrust the spikes of the shock pistol into Jerome's belly and fired. Electricity arced out from Jerome's limbs as he twitched violently from the paralysing energy coursing through his body. Gilbert, meanwhile, found himself psychologically paralysed. He watched in horror as Ulysses tossed Jerome over the side of the walkway.

Ulysses gave a deep, dark laugh, stomping with malicious deliberation toward Elena.

'So, what are you? Some sort of robot? Someone spent a lot of time putting you together. It will almost be a shame melting down that gold skin of yours. Such a pretty lass you are.'

'The title you are looking for is Lady,' she retorted calmly.

'What is it you're after up there, anyway? This whole place is made of gold; what could possibly be in there that could be any more valuable?' He was almost upon her then. 'I mean, I'm going to see soon enough, but I'd like to know what it is I'm looking for.'

'I'm sure a man of war, like yourself, wouldn't understand. It's why I came here; why the seven kingdoms of Atlantis followed me here.'

Elena stood unwavering, carefully watching Ulysses for any sudden movement. Then something caught her eye.

Riding up on one of the rotating rings was Jerome, clinging to a carved, gold-plated symbol. At the ring's apogee, he dropped back onto the walkway.

The sound made Ulysses spin around, hardly believing his eyes. Elena leapt forward, wrenching the shock pistol from his grasp. He swung a meaty fist wildly at her. Elena ducked, dodging the sloppy assault with ease. He looked back over his shoulder, remembering Jerome, just in time to see a flash of green. The four-inch hole in Ulysses' head smouldered as his body went limp and slumped to the ground.

Still sitting where he had stumbled earlier, Gilbert was furiously scratching away with his pen in his notebook.

'They'll think it's a joke,' he repeatedly muttered to himself as he wrote.

'Well, that was exciting.' Jerome flashed his standard toothy smile as he leaned on his cane. 'Wish I could have saved his goggles, though.'

Elena helped Gilbert to his feet.

'You're going to have to tell him now,' she said, looking back at Jerome.

He was running his hand over his slicked-back black hair, clearly not accustomed to being without his hat.

'I suppose the cat is out of the bag, as it were.'

Jerome walked up to the two of them with his usual calm swagger as he unbuttoned his vest with his free hand. The holes from the spikes of Ulysses' shock pistol were clearly visible in the grey vest, but bloodless.

'How are you still… Are you okay? Shouldn't you be bleeding or something?'

Gilbert was trying to gather his racing thoughts.

'I'm fine. I've certainly been through worse.' Jerome opened his vest.

His shirt had been burnt away and, shockingly, so too had much of the skin of his belly, exposing a collection of flexing tension coils, gears, springs, and the grey metal bones of the lower portion of his rib cage.

'Wait, you're mechanical too?'

Gilbert couldn't make sense of what he was looking at. He glanced back up at Jerome's face. He appeared utterly human.

'I'm a little older than you might think as well,' Jerome chuckled as he rebuttoned his vest. 'Though not nearly as old as…'

'No need to be rude now, Jerome,' Elena scolded, 'but you are some of Da Vinci's best work.'

Jerome nodded politely, surprised by the honest compliment.

'Shall we?' He motioned in the direction of the spherical

building.

'Yes, the time should be just right.' There was excitement in her voice.

'No one is going to believe any of it,' Gilbert muttered, now failing to muster the enthusiasm to write any further in his notebook.

The three of them entered the round building. Inside, the walkway split to the left and right, rejoining on the far side from the entrance, forming a suspended ring. The interior was a singular open space; the walls glowed a brilliant blue. A rotating stone ring, identical to the rings around the walkway outside but much smaller, floated vertically in the room's centre. In its centre, a small gold cube, no larger than a man's fist, was suspended just as magically as the stone ring. It spun gently in multiple directions. Its surface was covered in subtle intersecting circular and spiralling etchings.

Lady Saphuthest handed Gilbert the shock pistol and approached the ring. Reaching in ever so slowly, she gently cupped the gold cube in both hands, drawing it out from the ring. The walls of the room shifted to an orange glow.

'Really?' Gilbert said loudly, more than just a little exasperated. 'All of this for a block of gold? I don't understand. There are entire buildings of nothing but gold bricks out there. What makes this little block so special?'

Elena smiled. 'This is no block of gold,' she said, motioning with her head for the two men to gather closer.

As the two men gazed at the cube, subtle whirring sounds, clicks and snaps began emanating from the object. A moment later, the subtly etched lines deepened, dividing the cube into many complex panels. The panels started sliding apart and reconnecting in surprising new configurations, slowly altering the cube into new and unusual shapes. Occasionally, small, delicate gears could be seen frantically spinning away inside. Soon the cube had evolved into something vaguely egg-shaped and had nearly doubled in size. A few moments more, and Gilbert was stunned with awe. He could hardly believe it was possible that he could be more surprised than he had already been by the various revelations and wonders of the day. What just moments before had been a small gold cube was now a smooth, gold-skinned baby girl nestled in Elena's arms. It began to flounder and fuss. Its eyes were closed tight, just as a newborn human baby would. Elena was beaming.

'This is my daughter. She is my whole reason for building this city of love and harmony far from the conflicts of humankind. She has taken nearly ten thousand years to form, as my kind does. I was afraid I wouldn't be here in time. Thank you so much, Jerome. I will never be able to repay you properly.' A tear glinted down her gold cheek.

'Well, you could name your daughter after me,' Jerome offered. 'But I'm not sure Jerome works for a girl.'

'Quite,' Elena responded, giving Jerome a slightly scolding frown. 'My kind waits until our children are old enough to choose names for themselves. Until then, she is simply "Daughter".'

'Wait, you can cry? Can robots cry?'

Gilbert had a new barrage of questions welling up within him.

Jerome could sense it and intercepted the man.

'Now, now, let us leave the new mother to tend to her child. We really should head back to the Maeldun before Harriet sets off without us. I am the captain now, after all.'

'You're the – what now?' Gilbert questioned. 'I thought that Harriet woman...'

'I'll explain later,' Jerome said, leading Gilbert out of the building.

Trailing behind the other two, Elena chimed up, 'So, Captain,' the joy continuing to build in her voice. 'Where to now?'

'Well, we're still going to have to outrun the Cetus, but after that, there's something I need to tend to on the Moon. I have it on good authority that someone recently ventured to the Moon and back in nothing more than a hot air balloon. The Maeldun should be more than capable of making the trip.'

Jerome flashed his companions the broadest, most beguiling smile.

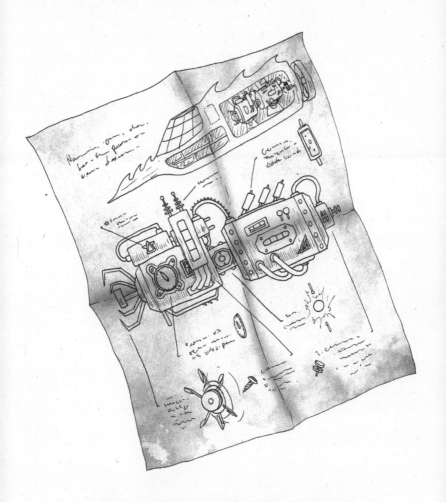

Corsair and The Sky
Pirates
by Mark Piggott

1887 **in the city of Amiens, France…** The port city in northern France was not a bustling seaport as it appeared to be, but rather a quiet, little community divided by the Somme. The sound of seagulls, steamship whistles, and church bells were as much noise as this tiny seaside community could manage. It's home to one of France's largest cathedrals and one of the world's greatest authors.

At a small café in Quartier St.-Leu, Jules Verne sipped quietly on his coffee as he sifted through the Paris newspaper. Verne enjoyed quiet moments like this. It helped clear his mind and arrange his thoughts for the next adventure he would bring to life.

You wouldn't know by looking at this quiet, little man that he was such a renowned author. His white hair and beard matched the wrinkles on his face. He rubbed his left leg regularly, hoping to relieve the pain. It still ached where his nephew, Gaston, once shot him. The poor boy was locked away in an asylum, with little to no explanation of why he did it. All that remained was the ache in his leg.

The pain was a constant reminder to Verne… A reminder of his mortality, and it scared him. He left behind a legacy in his stories of science, fantasy, and adventure, but was it enough, he wondered? Do these "flights of fancy" mean anything beyond the pages he wrote?

'*Pardon Moi, monsieur,*' came a voice, startling the author. 'Are you Jules Verne?'

He looked up from his newspaper to see a tall, skinny young man standing next to him. He bowed slightly at the waist with a bowler hat resting in his hand over his heart. Verne knew the young man had to be from Eastern Europe through his burly moustache and thick accent. His dark clothes reminded Verne of an undertaker. He hoped that was not the case.

'*Oui*, may I help you?' Verne asked.

'I am Nikola Tesla,' he said. 'I am a great admirer of your work, Monsieur Verne. I apologise for interrupting you, but your housekeeper said I might find you here. I was hoping I could have a moment of your time.'

Verne thought for a moment before nodding and motioning for him to sit down. Although Tesla hated engaging with admirers, he knew it was part of the fame of being an author. Tesla was thrilled and sat in the chair across from Verne. Before he could say anything, the waiter approached the two men.

'*Voulez-vous un café, monsieur?*' he asked Tesla.

'*Oui, merci,*' he replied. '*Et un verre d'eau s'il vous plait.*'

Tesla waited patiently for the waiter to depart before saying anything, but Verne spoke first.

'From your accent, I can assume you are from Eastern Europe, *Monsieur* Tesla. Austria or Hungary, am I correct?' Verne inquired.

'Serbia, *Monsieur* Verne, but it is part of the Austro-Hungarian Empire, so you are quite correct.'

'And what brings you to Amiens? Surely you did not come here just to get my autograph?' Verne quipped.

'*Non, Monsieur...*' Tesla started to say, 'I work for the Continental Edison Company. I came to Amiens to work on the electrical system. I thought I might get the chance to speak with you before I return to Paris.'

'Edison... Well, well, I must thank you for the electric lights,' Verne commended. 'It is better to light the night with your electric light bulb than to try to write by candlelight at three o'clock in the morning.'

Tesla smiled and nodded in appreciation of the compliment.

'Thank you, *Monsieur* Verne, but perhaps I can inspire you in another way,' Tesla remarked as he pulled out a folded piece of paper from his coat and handed it to Verne.

'*Qu'est-ce que c'est?*' he asked. 'I thought you weren't looking for my autograph.'

'No, no… this is something that your writings inspired me to create.'

He piqued Verne's curiosity as he carefully unfolded the paper. When he saw what was inside, his eyes grew as large as hen's eggs. It was an engine. One so complicated in design that Verne could not understand the intricacies of what he was seeing. Around the machine was a crude drawing of a ship, a submersible ship that resembled his Nautilus description.

'*Incroyable,*' Verne whispered, amazed at what he saw. 'What is it?'

'A steam-powered oscillating electrical generator,' Tesla explained. 'It can generate twenty times the electrical power of anything produced today, maybe more. My machine could power a ship, like your Nautilus, don't you think?'

'*En effet…* indeed it could, but it would take a ton of coal just to generate the amount of steam you would need to power such an engine, wouldn't you agree?'

'Under normal circumstances, yes, but not with this,' Tesla said.

He looked around first to see if anyone was watching him before he reached into his pocket and pulled out a small, corked test tube. Inside was a few small blue stones that glowed dimly in the morning light. He handed it to Verne, who stared at them in awe.

'What on earth are they?' Verne asked.

'They're from a meteor that fell near my home in Serbia, near the Balkans,' Tesla began to explain. He abruptly stopped when the waiter returned with his coffee and a glass of water, as he requested. He waited until the waiter departed to continue his explanation. 'It generates a constant heat that never seems to die out. Here, please observe...'

Tesla took the cork off the test tube vial and poured one of the small meteorite fragments into the glass of water. The blue rock began to bubble and burn, raising the water's temperature rapidly. Soon, the water was boiling as steam arose from the glass. Tesla took a spoon and pulled out the tiny rock before dropping it carefully on the table.

'You can pick it up, *Monsieur*. It won't burn you.'

Verne reached down and tentatively touched it with his fingertips until he realised how cool the rock was. He picked it up and held it in his hand.

'*Monsieur* Tesla, this is quite, well... *remarquable!*'

'It expends energy without any reduction in its size or mass,' Tesla boasted proudly. 'It could change the world as we know it.'

'Is there any more of this meteor?' Verne asked. 'Where does it come from?'

'I have a colleague at the Royal Astrological Society in England who discovered a comet he named Uriel, after the archangel,' Tesla explained. 'As the comet passed by our planet, Uriel's fragments impacted the earth from the Urals to the Alps and across North America. We are working on a method to detect the fragments of the meteorite. So far, I've collected nearly 500 kilograms.'

'You are an incredibly talented young man, *Monsieur* Tesla,' Verne said as he handed him the meteor, dropping it into the tube. Verne then folded the paper and gave it back. 'But what does this have to do with an old man like me? I am a writer of flights of fancy, not a scientist.'

'Your stories have inspired me to pursue new avenues of science. You have dared to dream the impossible, but this,' Tesla said as he held up the test tube. 'This makes it possible. I would like to collaborate with you on some ideas that I have. I have the scientific knowledge, and you have an incredible imagination. Perhaps, together, we can bring about a new age of science and technology; one that benefits all of humanity.'

'Won't that interfere with your work at the Edison Company?' Verne asked.

'I have already put in my notice to leave my position with Edison,' Tesla explained. 'I am planning to go to the United States and pursue my dreams there, but before I go, I wanted to work with you on my designs. Besides,' he continued, 'I don't want my ideas to come under an Edison patent instead of my own. He is a brilliant man, but his ambitions are to pursue science for wealth. I cannot be a part of that. Something like this,' he said, shaking his design at Verne as he picked it up, 'could change the course of human history. It just needs a little imagination to make it come true. You, *Monsieur* Verne, are a master of imagination. Imagine what we could accomplish together?'

Verne sat there, intrigued by the young man's offer. For the first time, he saw how his novels could influence mankind's future.

'Very well, *Monsieur* Tesla. Where do we begin?'

*

1907, somewhere over the English Channel… The storm raged over the rolling seas, with fierce winds creating a pounding surf as thunder and lightning roared in the overcast sky. It takes skilled pilots to navigate these storms, on the sea, and in the air.

Murky fog usually shrouded any visibility. It was a potential hazard for any ship daring to sail these waters, but not this ship. Above the waves and crashing seas, floating effortlessly in the air, the zeppelin *Valiant* sailed toward Great Britain.

The *Valiant* was the pinnacle of first-class accommodations for passengers travelling throughout the British Empire. With an Edison Counter-Oscillation Engine, the majestic zeppelin could stay airborne indefinitely, providing its guests with every luxury imaginable. At nearly 1,200 feet in length, the *Valiant* was the pride of the White Star fleet of airships. The rigid frame was adorned with gold and brass fittings, emulating its rich beginnings. It could carry more than 200 passengers with a complement of 300 officers, crew, and staff to tend to their every need.

Thanks to the genius and unparalleled vision of inventors like Tesla, Edison, Alexander Graham Bell, Elijah McCoy, and others, steam-powered machines utilising Uriel's comet's fragments were bringing about an industrial revolution like the world had never seen. The *Valiant* was an example of this incredible new age.

Such a prize was also very tempting for those who would challenge the rich and powerful authority, and there was one word for them: Pirates. Even in these modern times, brigands took to the skies to fight for the oppressed through cunning and guile, a calling answered by Corsair and his Sky Pirates.

Above the cloud line, moving in over the *Valiant*, was another airship. This one was smaller, but relatively well-armed. Dual-barrel cannons adorned the top, sides, and underneath, rotating around the dirigible frame on a track. The dirigible's rigid structure was covered in sectioned armour plating to protect it from harm. They painted the blimp to resemble a rainbow-striped serpent, with sharp teeth and an intimidating grin flowing aft as its body wrapped around the dirigible. On the tail fin of the airship was the traditional skull and crossbones, denoting its pirate allegiance.

The blimp was the *Galeru*, and it belonged to one of the most infamous pirates of this age, Corsair. The daring deeds of this sky pirate and his crew made him a villain to authorities and a celebrity to the people. In an age of modern marvels, the wealthy grew richer off the workers' backs, toiling in the factories worldwide to produce these wondrous inventions for people, but at the cost of human lives. Corsair was a new age "Robin Hood," robbing from the wealthy and affluent and giving it to the poor and those in need, but there was more to him than being a thief and a pirate. He kept his secrets close, and only those he trusted most knew what they were.

On the bridge of the *Galeru*, first officer Francesca "Kiki" Mori peered out at the *Valiant* through her spyglass. Her long, black hair was pulled back in a traditional Japanese bun called a Shimada, held up with ornate oriental combs and hairpins. Her appearance and style showed off her adoptive homeland's Japanese heritage with a modern take on samurai armour layered over her Victorian sensibilities. She considered herself a *Ronin* or a samurai without a master. With a katana around her waist and a Colt M1895 strapped to her hip, Kiki was an intimidating presence. Her skill as a swordswoman was one of many hidden talents that made her an asset to Corsair.

'Keep her steady, Eager! We want to stay right in her blind spot!' she ordered.

Behind her, at the helm, Gelar "Eager" Kingsman kept a tight grip on the ship's wheel. The old aboriginal looked nothing like a modern navigator. His baggy clothes covered his thin, bony frame, and consisted of a short-sleeved shirt and shorts. He said he needed his skin exposed like that to feel the slightest shift in the air around him and the movement of the ship under his feet. His white hair and beard were quite long, stringy, and somewhat unkempt. The goggles he wore over his eyes had white lenses to hide that he was blind. Although he couldn't see the world around him, Eager had an unnatural ability to pilot the *Galeru*, which is why Corsair kept him on board. His other senses were so sensitive; he could "see" the world better than the rest of us.

'Don't you worry none, Lady Kiki. We're right where we want to be,' he replied in a thick Aboriginal accent, exuding confidence. 'Their radio wave detector is focused forward, monitoring the storm. Back aft, they're as blind as I am.'

She looked at the *Valiant* again with her spyglass, spying along the top for any lookout or guards keeping watch. Most of these first-class zeppelins had lookout towers and guard posts along the top centre line. These domed viewing posts were visible along the dirigible spine, raised and lower in inclement weather. Kiki could see that they were all closed and locked down.

'It looks like their top deck lookout posts are down, but why would they do that?' Kiki asked. 'Even in this weather, they always keep one operational... it's standard procedure. Why on earth would they risk it?'

'They wouldn't...' said a voice behind her.

He stepped on the bridge of the *Galeru* with the confidence of a commander. His long, leather waistcoat covered a bronze-metal inlaid vest that hugged his body tight. He had a twin modified Colt M1895 strapped around his waist and a cutlass at his side. The sword's guard and hilt wrapped around in moving gears, leaving one to imagine what power it held within. A flowing red scarf wrapped around his neck, fluttering around as he walked. His shoulder-length black hair was pushed back off his face by a large pair of optics. His handsome face gleamed with a devilish grin that made most women swoon. No one knew his real name, only the name he went by... Corsair.

'No guards or lookouts means only one thing, Kiki,' he said as he stepped up next to her. 'They're guarding something so valuable they can't afford to spare anyone for lookout duty.'

'Private security? Pinkertons, maybe?' she asked. 'Do you think they're transporting some pieces of the comet?'

'According to my sources, yes...' Corsair said as he lowered his optics over his eyes. He turned some dials to extend the lenses outward, giving him a better view of the *Valiant*. 'And it's not just that, Kiki. Our spies saw John Kruesi getting on board in Paris.'

'Edison's right hand? What's he doing on this side of the Atlantic?' Kiki inquired.

'That's what we're here to find out,' Corsair said as he continued to look out over the *Valiant*.

'More security means we'll need bigger guns,' Kiki replied. 'This one could get messy, Captain.'

'No doubt,' Corsair confirmed. 'But every world government is trying to find as much of that meteorite as they can for ERP, and they'll stop at nothing to get their hands on it.'

ERP, the Edison/Röntgen/Parsons Corporation, was the leading designer for many fantastic machines and engines that the world had never seen. From motion pictures to phonographs, electrical power generators to weapons of war, ERP supplied them all. Their hands reached deep into the pockets of all the major world powers, from America and Great Britain to Germany and Russia.

'Just so they can keep their factories running 24/7, running the poor and destitute into the ground while they relax in luxury,' Kiki interrupted. 'Bastards!'

'Get the crew ready; we drop in twenty…' Corsair ordered. Kiki ran off the bridge to get the rest of the crew ready to board the *Valiant*. 'Eager, when I give the signal, bring us down to 15 feet above the *Valiant*, just past the tailfin.'

'Roger 'oy *gubba*!' Eager cajoled, calling the Corsair his "little boy," as he always did.

Even though over two-thirds of the *Galeru* was open space for helium bladders, the lower two decks were crew areas. The largest of them was the hangar bay. It held two small aircrafts called aero-wings. Two bicycle shop owners designed it in Ohio using a Tesla engine, along with retractable gun mounts and a bomb rack. It also contained several drop tubes – hydraulic cylinders that forced their way into the superstructure of another airship – allowing for quick boarding and an equally fast escape.

Corsair's crew gathered around the hangar, checking their weapons for the upcoming raid. According to their criminal records, these men and women were assorted low-lives, scoundrels, and thieves from the four corners of the globe. Those records didn't reflect the deep commitment they had for the people who needed their help and fully supported Corsair's cause. Many of them lived for the thrill of the hunt, the adventure, and the payoff after a good heist. They say, "no honour among thieves," but this group was the exception.

'Knox, why the hell are you taking that cannon? This bunch of snotty, fancy-pants *Stronzo* down there, not the Kaiser's *Eisenwand*... No?' said Eddie "Dash" Castello, who was trimming his wispy thin moustache as he gazed into a small hand mirror.

The little Italian didn't look it, but he was the weapons/demolitions expert aboard the *Galeru*; a regular deadeye for his accuracy with anything from a long gun to a pea shooter. Aboard the airship, they called him Dash because of how fast he picked up on things. He started using explosives in the *Carbosulcis* Coal Mine at age 10. Dash's experiences and hardships there made him quite eager to take to the skies when he met Corsair.

He always looked overburdened with an assortment of weapons and explosives strapped to his belt, thighs, back, and bandoliers across his chest. To him, it was like wearing his favourite sweater. Next to Corsair, Dash was the best shot in the crew.

'The Captain said to expect the worst, so I always come prepared,' replied Heinrich "Knox" Romig.

The armoured soldier carefully loaded the ammunition feeder into his .58 calibre Gatling gun. He kept the massive weapon slung over his shoulder with the ammunition fed from a huge backpack. Knox was a former member of the Kaiser's elite *Eisenwand*. They were German special forces that wore steam-powered armour under long coats, making them practically invincible. His head was cleanly shaven, but a thick, burly beard covered his jawline. He towered over Dash and most of the crew and looked as if he could toss a bear with ease. They called him Knox after "Fort Knox" because he was impregnable in body and spirit.

Knox was one of the most decorated soldiers in the *Eisenwand*, until the day his superiors ordered him to lead an attack against insurgents in an abandoned factory in Poland. However, that factory turned out to be an orphanage full of children. After that slaughter, he left his chest full of medals and joined Corsair.

'Besides, I have to protect everyone. Even you, Dash,' Knox said as he hoisted his gun across his shoulder.

'That is always refreshing to hear, my dear Heinrich,' cooed Felicia Scarlett "Fox" Bertrand, in her quaint British accent.

Fox sat comfortably; her legs were crossed while she continued with her manicure. Her form-fitting dress didn't seem appropriate for a raid, even though her red hair was pulled up tight into a bun and her make-up was immaculately done. Fox – better known as the "Scarlett Fox" in most circles – was a Shade, a spy, and an expert on infiltration and information collecting. Her beauty, charm, and ability to blend into any environment made her an asset in more ways than one. Her skills were once the British Secret Intelligence Service's pride, but she left shortly after discovering how deep ERP was into the British government. After British Intelligence framed her for murder, Fox met Corsair and found a new purpose in life.

'You know I will always have your back, *mia adorabile signora!*' Dash said as he leaned into her and twirled his moustache. 'And what a lovely backside it is!'

In a blur, Fox pulled out a dagger hidden in her belt and spun it around her fingertips until she placed the tip of the blade under his chin.

'Comment about my backside again, Dash, and your front side will get my full attention.'

Dash just ignored her threats until a strong hand grabbed him by the scruff of his neck and pulled him back.

'Dash, you're one second away from Fox giving you a butcher's Sunday special,' said Henry "Bronx" Jones. 'When are you gonna learn to leave that woman alone?' Bronx, a black garage mechanic from New York City, was the chief engineer on the Galeru. Bronx was a natural when it came to engines, especially the complex Tesla Oscillating Electric Engines. He was known by many as a Vernian. He studied mechanical engineering, but he also read Jules Verne's novels and – like Tesla – he put his ideas to practise. For a black man in America, that was a hard-fought education he learned from behind the scenes. He worked as a mechanic by day and as a janitor at a major university by night. He would study the textbooks and chalkboards as he cleaned the rooms, getting a college education on his own time.

'Never, *mi Amico*,' Dash replied. 'She has the key to my heart.'

'She's going to shove those keys up your backside one of these days,' Bronx snapped back. 'Besides, Captain's on his way down.'

Just as Bronx said, Corsair and Kiki stepped down the spiral staircase leading from the bridge into the hangar and the team's last member. Like the rest of this mismatched crew of infamy, Nathanial "Moon Crow" Potomac was no exception. He was a proud Apache warrior from the plains of the American Southwest. The sole survivor of the American soldiers' massacre, Moon Crow was rescued by a frontier family heading west. Although they gave him a proper English name, he never lost sight of his Apache roots. He took the name Moon Crow from a story his adopted family told him. They found him on a moonlit night, holding onto a dead crow. He saw that as a sign – a vision quest. His destiny laid beyond his tribe.

He dressed like a modern man – button-down shirt, vest, and pants – with a few exceptions that emulated his heritage. Centred on a bolo tie around his collar was a large turquoise stone, a piece of his homeland he carried. On a wide-brimmed hat that he wore on his head, crow feathers with white tips protruded on the side, held in place by a band of multi-coloured beads that he wove himself. The white tips represented the moon in the night sky. A pair of tomahawks dangled from his belt with an 1894 Winchester repeating rifle slung across his back.

'Alright, you knockers, gather round and listen up,' Kiki shouted to get their attention.

Everyone moved in around Corsair to get their debriefing before the drop. It always excited them when a new job approached, but they never strayed from Corsair's orders. His word was absolute.

'So, what's the plan, *Mi Amico*... Burn it down or smash and grab?' Dash joked.

Bronx slapped him on the back of the head for his lack of decorum in front of the captain.

'Smash and grab, Dash, but with a purpose,' Corsair said. 'We've got two targets, and we need to get in and out as quickly as possible with the least amount of collateral damage. That means leave the passengers alone this time. We don't have the time for our normal "Robin Hood" routine.'

'You sound worried, *Kapitän*,' Knox observed.

'Not worried, Knox, just cautious. I have faith in my crew to do the job,' he said with a smile as he looked around at everyone. 'But this is no ordinary heist. There are more than just your normal White Star security guards this time around. With Kruesi aboard, there's probably Pinkerton's on his private security detail. So, you know what that means?'

'Shoot to kill,' Fox interjected. 'Those mercenaries don't play around.'

Corsair pointed right at her. 'Exactly, so let's split up into two teams and hit them hard and fast. Kiki... you, Knox, and Dash will head aft. The piece of Uriel's comet is yours. Find it and get it back to the *Galeru*. Bronx, you, and Moon Crow, are with me. We're going after Kruesi.'

'And what about *Signora* Scarlett? Why can't she be on my team?' Dash asked with a wink at Fox.

She just shook her head, not even bothering to look at him when she spoke.

'I have my mission, Eddie darling, one that does not include you!'

'Alright then, lock and load, charge up your gear, and get ready to drop... Five minutes!' Corsair ordered as everyone made their final preps and geared up for the drop.

Kiki didn't like what she heard from Fox and confided in the captain.

'Why is the Fox going solo? I thought we discussed this and decided it was a bad idea?' she queried.

'We did, but then Scarlett convinced me it was a good idea,'

Corsair snipped back while he loaded his Colt revolver. He didn't even look up at her, which made Kiki scowl.

'Yeah, I bet she convinced you...'

'Kiki,' he interrupted her scathing retort. 'Fox is familiar with the *Valiant* class of airship. She knows all the hiding places the first-class passengers use to hide away their secrets. If there's someone or something else aboard, I want to know about it, and Scarlett has the best... assets to discover them for us.'

'It's not her assets that I'm worried about,' Kiki argued. 'I don't like it when one of the team goes solo. I may not like that "ginger" fox, but I don't want her dead or captured either.'

'Why Kiki, you do care!' Fox surprised her from behind, her wicked smile and fluttering eyelashes professing her sarcasm. 'I knew that deep down, you loved me!'

'Love, no... loath, yes!' Kiki groaned as she stormed away in a huff. Corsair wanted to laugh, but he kept it inside.

'Now, Scarlett, that wasn't very nice,' he scolded her. 'But Kiki does have a point. It would be best if you didn't take any unnecessary risks. If it gets hairy, you get out of there, understand?'

'Things never get hairy with me, my darling Corsair,' Kiki retorted as she dragged her finger under Corsair's chin, slowly and seductively. 'That's why I shave my legs... So, I can get out of those tight situations.'

As she walked away toward her drop tube, Dash watched her walk with his eyes wide open. '*Buon Dio, Sono Innamorato!*' he exclaimed, professing his love for the femme fatal.

Knox just lifted him by his collar and carried him over to their drop tube. Dash was dangling in the air as he tried to get away from the brute.

Corsair chuckled aloud this time. He loved his team and would do anything for them; he would die for them. He went over to the internal communication pod next to his drop tube and flicked the switch to talk.

'Okay, Eager, move us in position and drop when ready.'

'Roger 'oy *gubba*! Two minutes to drop!' Eager shouted through the speaker box.

Everyone stepped into their drop tubes. The metal cylinders, about the size of a typical elevator, could comfortably fit three to four people. Their size was one of the reasons Corsair always put Dash with Knox. Between the two of them, they equalled out to three people. Even with Kiki, it was still going to be a tight fit.

Once everyone got situated inside their cylinder, the doors closed. A sheath of canvas threaded with metal rings extended down and around the tube. The trapdoors beneath them slid open. There was a hiss of steam escaping as the iris unfurled, allowing the wind and rain to rush in from the outside.

'Hold on to your lunches, ladies and gents,' Eager yelled out from the bridge. 'Dropping in 3… 2… and 1!'

With the flick of a switch, Eager sent the tubes down into the airship below. Hydraulic springs forced them through the superstructure and canvas covering the top of the zeppelin, driving them onto the airships' upper platform.

All the world's airships were similarly designed. There was an upper catwalk right along the centre line to allow personnel to inspect the top of the superstructure, check for leaks in the helium bladders, man lookout positions, etc. Once in place, the cylinders hooked onto the catwalks, keeping them steady and locked in for an easy entry or exit as the canvas retracted to the top of the superstructure. They're also self-sealed to keep the elements out, so the targets are unaware that they've been boarded.

Once the drop process finished, the cylinder doors opened, and everyone jumped out, looking for trouble.

'Pirates!' a voice shouted from down the catwalk.

Everyone looked to see a maintenance man running away, shouting out the warning. Without even thinking, Moon Crow took out a tomahawk and threw it at the frightened crewmember. His aim was perfect, hitting him squarely in the back of the head. He was dead before he hit the ground.

Corsair and his crew knew that a stray bullet could set off the helium inside this part of the zeppelin. That's why edged weapons were best in the upper reaches of the airship. Corsair motioned for the two groups to take off without saying a word. No one knew if anyone heard the dead man's warning. Kiki and her team headed aft while Corsair and his group headed forward. Fox found the first available ladder off the catwalk and started to descend.

Moon Crow pulled out the tomahawk and wiped off the blood in the dead man's hair. He didn't say a word; he never did in battle. In his opinion, words wasted energy. As they continued forward, Bronx looked around in awe at the mechanics of a zeppelin like the *Valiant*.

'Geez, Captain, you sure you can't do this without me? I'd sure like to get my hands on one of these Röntgen Inertia Stabilisers. It might help to keep the *Galeru* flying straight.'

'That's why we've got Eager. Sorry, Bronx, but I need you to focus your "Vernian" mind on something new,' Corsair explained. 'Kruesi is said to have one of those new Hollerith Thinking Machines with him. I need you to tell me whether or not this is something worth stealing.'

'Oh, I've been dying to get a look at one of those,' Bronx anticipated with childlike glee.

'Okay, okay, for now, tap into the communications grid and find that bastard for me.'

Moon Crow led them to a junction box, and Bronx immediately got to work. His backpack was not filled with tools but rather electronics… specifically a Tesla Radiographic Frequency Modulator or R.F.M. With it, Bronx could tap into the ship's electrical grid to create a visual of everyone and everything on board using his goggles. They had an internal radar which uses the electrical impulses of the airship.

Bronx got a good look around with his oversized goggles covering his face. In his optics, they appeared as patterns – a series of blips and squiggles to the average viewer – but to a Vernian like Bronx, it was as clear as day. He adjusted the dials on his goggles to follow the electrical impulses as they moved around the airship. He saw passengers enjoy fine dining on the main promenade; crew members were keeping them satisfied, tending to their every need, from the waiters to the housekeepers. The ship's security were making their routine patrols. He even spied Scarlett moving behind the scenes with ease and watched Kiki's team descend into the cargo hold.

Finally, he found what Corsair wanted. In the *Valiant's* nose was a first-class cabin usually reserved for politicians and royalty… In this case, a member of the majesty of industry. Several brutes surrounded the nose cone cabin, both in and out. They were protecting a single individual. Bronx also noted a larger than usual electrical power surge in this cabin. There was no doubt; John Kruesi was here.

'Got him, Captain, but there's at least a dozen of those Pinkerton goons around him,' Bronx reported.

'That's okay, Bronx. I've got a plan to get us in there.'

*

The Pinkertons were the best security money could buy. They were well-trained, better than most armies, and equally well-equipped. Failure was not an option for those who wore the Pinkerton badge. They all dressed the same, too: Wide-brimmed fedora hats, highly polished boots, and suit coats cut a little bit bigger than average to accommodate the bulletproof vest they wore underneath. It made them all look bulky and broad-chested. They carried Colt M1900 automatic weapons or the new Remington Model 8 semi-automatic rifles. Anyone who would attempt to confront them would be outgunned, outmatched, and usually, outclassed.

There was silence in the corridor. Nobody spoke so that they could focus on their job and be alert for anything out of the ordinary. The squeaky wheel of a cart rolling across the floor snapped them to attention. The six men tightened their grip on their weapons, ready to strike back if necessary.

Bronx, dressed like a waiter, pushed the cart down the corridor. It was a simple serving cart, covered with a white tablecloth. On top was a bottle of champagne chilling in an ice bucket with glasses and a metal dome covering something delectable. The lead Pinkerton held up his hand to stop him from approaching any further.

'Hold it right there, boy. This area is off limits. Besides, we didn't order anything.'

'No, sir. I'm sorry, sir, but the Captain sent this up for Mister Kruesi,' Bronx answered, faking his best imitation of a British accent. 'Champagne and caviar, with his compliments!'

The Pinkerton officer looked suspiciously at Bronx and everything on the cart. He lifted the dome, visually inspecting the contents, checked underneath the tablecloth covering the cart, and made sure everything was on the up-and-up. Even then, it didn't convince him.

'Why don't we call up to the bridge and ask the captain about this,' he said with a wicked grin as he stepped over to the intercom box.

'I understand, sir. Go right ahead. Take all the time you need. It saves me from having to get back to the kitchen and help do the dishes,' Bronx replied with a laugh.

The Pinkerton thought for a minute as he reached for the switch, but the more he thought, the more his blood boiled.

'Go on, boy. Get back to the kitchen and get those dishes done. I'm sure it's all your good for,' he quipped.

Bronx didn't say a word as the smile slipped from his face. He just turned around and left the cart behind. The Pinkerton walked back, laughing as he reached for the bottle of champagne.

'Since Mr Kruesi didn't order this, I guess we should check it out, for poison, I mean. Don't you think?' he said as the men around him laughed and agreed with him wholeheartedly.

But when he lifted the bottle from the ice bucket, all hell broke loose. An explosion of steam erupted from inside the bucket, but instead of burning everyone in scalding water, it had a very different effect. The billowing mist froze everything it touched, from the walls and floors to the men in the room. They found themselves encased in a layer of ice, unable to move or even breathe.

From down the corridor, Corsair approached the frozen Pinkertons with Moon Crow and Bronx. Bronx was changing out of the waiter's uniform back into his working clothes. He walked up to the frozen Pinkerton, who chastised him. He was still holding the champagne bottle, now frozen.

'This is what I'm good at,' Bronx started to explain through the icy exterior. 'It's called "adiabatic reversible expansion"… steam held under high pressure when released, absorbs the heat from everything around it, freezing it solid. I packed a steam ball into the ice bucket because I knew a greedy snob like you would want to keep it for yourself.'

Corsair let Bronx rant at the frozen Pinkerton. He knew of the hard life he had just because of his skin colour. He hated seeing his friend treated that way, which is why he did what he did.

The men reached the door to the suite, covered in a layer of ice. Corsair didn't even hesitate when he kicked the door in and attacked. There were four Pinkertons with Kruesi. Even though they outnumbered them, that never mattered to Corsair.

The sky pirate shot two of the men in their legs, causing them to fall over and grab their injuries. Moon Crow threw his two tomahawks with precision, hitting the other two Pinkertons in the neck, killing them instantly. While Bronx disarmed the two wounded Pinkertons, Corsair approached the only man still in the room. He levelled his cutlass at him, placing the tip of his blade underneath his chin.

He sat quietly, so as not to agitate anyone, holding his teacup and saucer just below Corsair's blade. His hair was slicked back, framing his face neatly, but you couldn't tell that by the bushy beard and moustache that covered his jawline. He dressed immaculately for a man in his position. He was John Kruesi, second in command at ERP and best friend of Thomas Edison.

Corsair stepped back, keeping his sword levelled at his throat, even as he sat down in the chair across from him.

'You're looking quite well, *Herr* Kruesi. Especially since you survived your bout of influenza, what… nearly ten years ago, wasn't it? It took you some time to recover. I hear the doctors in your home country of Switzerland are quite excellent.'

'*Da*, they are… I go back for a check-up from time to time,' he said as he took another sip of his tea. 'But I'm sure you know that, *Kapitän* Corsair.'

It impressed Corsair that Kreusi knew who he was. He should have expected it of Edison's second-in-command.

'Moon Crow, watch the door. Bronx, the machine should be on his desk. Check it out while *Herr* Kreusi and I have a little chat.'

Moon Crow locked the door and stood by it while Bronx jumped at the chance to check out the machine on Kruesi's desk. The ERP executive watched as Corsair's men followed his every word with such precision as he continued to sip his tea.

'I must say, you are exactly as I pictured you… Commanding in every sense of the word,' Kruesi said. 'But this adventure of yours is quite the folly. Do you think you can stop the world from advancing into a new age of industry and technology with these… heists?'

'I have no problem with the industrial revolution Tesla and Edison started, but not at the cost of the people you walk over as ERP lines their pockets with money,' Corsair retorted. 'Some of your inventions help and entertain everyday people, but not all of them. Only the ones who can pay your price, and the governments that will help usher in a world war.'

Those words caught Kruesi off guard, but he tried his best to hide any reaction.

'We provide weapons and munitions to many governments, for self-defence only.'

'Self-defence? Self-defence!' Corsair screamed as he stood up and moved his blade through the beard and onto the throat of Kruesi, causing him to drop his teacup. 'You call this self-defence?'

Corsair reached into his coat pocket and pulled out a folded photograph, throwing it at Kruesi.

He picked it up and looked at it, becoming nauseous at what he saw. Kruesi held one hand over his mouth, trying to prevent himself from throwing up. The picture showed naked bodies lying in a mass grave while soldiers stood over them, shooting down into the open grave, killing anyone still alive. It was a horrific sight to see.

'One of my Shades smuggled that photo out of the Ottoman Empire. I carry it as a reminder of what I'm fighting for. It was taken in Armenia, in a small town near the Caucasus mountain range. The town doesn't have a name anymore because you wiped it out, clearing the way to build a new ERP factory. One that specialises in something called Cobalt High Energy weapons.'

'Where did you hear that?' Kruesi interrupted, flinging the photograph at him.

He quickly found himself silenced by Corsair's blade. The sky pirate just smiled.

'I didn't really, just rumours mind you, but you just confirmed it,' he said as he picked up the photograph and put it back in his pocket. 'We heard bits and pieces, but we couldn't put it all together until now. You're using remnants of Uriel to power these new weapons, aren't you?'

'Of course, we are!' Kruesi snapped at Corsair, not holding back anymore. 'Using them to create steam, like Tesla, is mere child's play. Röntgen found out the true secret of Uriel, and with it, we will change the face of the world forever!'

'By building weapons that can destroy an entire city in a single blast by releasing the power of Uriel at the atomic level using Cobalt radioisotopes… An atomic bomb, I believe Röntgen called it.'

Kruesi couldn't believe what he was hearing. Someone exposed these closely guarded secrets of ERP, and all he could do was question where and how they learned about it.

'But to see if he's right, you needed to take your Hollerith Thinking Machine to work out the math,' Corsair continued. 'That's why you're here. Not for your health, but to do the final calculations; because Edison can't trust anyone with this but his right-hand man.'

Kruesi couldn't believe that this pirate could work out so much with very little information.

'I see your reputation proceeds you, *Kapitän* Corsair. You are indeed as clever as they say.'

'Oh, I'm not the smart one… He is,' Corsair said, nodding towards Bronx. 'How's it going, Bronx?'

'This machine is everything they said it was, Captain,' Bronx said as he stared at the wondrous machine in front of him.

He typed on a keypad that resembled a typewriter as he stared intently at the glass screen displaying the data. An Edison projector connected to a large console projected the image on the glass. The console was where data cards were fed in and out of the machine. They recorded and calculated the data.

Kruesi was amazed at how easily this young black man operated the complex thinking machine. He questioned his own bias toward their race; it was undeserving as he watched Bronx manipulate data strokes of the thinking machine with ease.

'There's good news and bad news, Captain,' Bronx said. 'The good news is this machine is amazing, and we should take it. I can imagine something like it running the entire ship one day.'

'And the bad news?' Corsair queried.

'The bad news is, without the data punch cards he used for his initial calculations, we may never know what he was trying to do in Armenia.'

'Then perhaps I can help, Bronx, dear,' came a sultry voice from the doorway. Moon Crow opened the door, and in walked the infamous Scarlett Fox. She was carrying a small sachet in her hand. 'I found this in the captain's safe. It seems even Mr Kruesi doesn't trust the pursers safe for his personal items. I thought I should bring it up here right away as you might need it, Corsair.'

She handed Bronx the sachet. When he opened the envelope, Bronx smiled as he pulled out the data punch cards.

'We got them, Captain,' Bronx said.

Corsair was happy until he saw the look on Kruesi's face. He was smirking, something John Kruesi would never do, especially at a time like this. Something was off, and Corsair knew it.

'Bronx, check on the others… quickly!' he ordered.

Bronx didn't hesitate as he plugged in the R.F.M. and lowered his goggles. It took him less than a minute to see why Kruesi was smiling like the cat that ate the canary.

'Captain, they've got a B.O.S.S. unit in the cargo hold!' Bronx said.

B.O.S.S., or Brute Omnipresent Steam Soldier, was the finest mechanical soldier that ERP ever invented. These monsters were loaded to bear with Gatling guns, Howitzer cannons, and a backpack mortar launcher. It was powered by a small yet powerful Edison Oscillating D/C Generator. It was a walking tank, resembling a giant or ogre of legend, and to bring one aboard a civilian airship was dangerous, even for ERP.

'Bronx, get this machine back aboard the *Galeru*. Fox, help him after you deal with this miscreant,' Corsair ordered. 'Moon Crow and I are heading aft!'

Without another word, he took off with his Apache compatriot leading the way. After they left, Fox looked at John Kruesi with a wicked grin as she pursed her lips.

'Now then, whatever shall I do with you, little man?' Kruesi swallowed hard.

***

The cargo hold of the *Valiant* was complete chaos. Automatic weapon fire rang out as bullets bounced around the room. On one side were several Pinkertons and the B.O.S.S., a two-person behemoth with a pilot and an engineer. The pilot controlled the mech, including movement and firing the weapons. Simultaneously, the engineer kept the steam pressure operating the complex systems under control and the ammunition flowing into the guns. Pipes, gears, and hoses moved the mech, acting like a human frame with arms and legs, but under mechanical operation.

Across the way, the constant fire pinned Kiki and her team down behind cargo crates and stacks of luggage. A hailstorm of bullets rang out, tearing through everything with no regard for personal property damage. That's why these airship lines had insurance for situations like these, especially when it came to pirates.

Kiki braced herself against the luggage rack, Colt revolver in one hand and her katana in the other. She looked across from her, watching Knox and Dash bracing themselves against the onslaught of firepower.

'We can't stay back here forever, *Fraulein* Kiki,' Knox shouted over the gunfire. 'That *verdammte maschine* is indestructible.'

'Except behind the knees,' Kiki said. 'That's why all their firepower is forward-facing.'

'Ah, then leave it to me, *Signora*!' Dash countered. 'Knox, I need a distraction.'

Knox knew just what Dash wanted. He stood straight up and opened fire, blasting back at the B.O.S.S. Although it barely scratched the surface, it did cause the Pinkertons to scatter. He took the brunt in his armoured chest plate while Dash quickly went to work. He peaked around Knox's massive legs, using him for protection while he set up his shot. If there was one thing Dash was good at, it was a trick ricochet shot. He loved the new Western motion pictures, always thinking he was a cowboy trying to outsmart the villain to save a damsel in distress. Besides that, you never wanted to play him in a game of pool.

After a few good looks, he squared up and aimed with his Colt revolver. It took seconds for him to fire, bouncing the bullet off some piping as it hit the B.O.S.S. behind its right knee. His shot was near perfect, breaking a hydraulic line, spraying fluid all around it. The slippery mess caused the Pinkertons hiding behind the monstrosity to fall to the ground, leaving them open to Knox's barrage as he adjusted his firing to cut them down, one-by-one. The B.O.S.S. unit went down to one knee and was forced to use its gun-arm to prop itself up. It appeared to be over until the pilot raised its other arm to fire. This one had a different weapon from the Gatling gun; it was a 7.5cm Howitzer canon. ERP didn't design it for use in an enclosed space like the cargo hold, but the B.O.S.S. pilot didn't care.

'*Dame Dayo,*' Kiki swore in Japanese when she saw the robotic soldier aiming the cannon at them.

She froze in fear and thought this was the end until he arrived. Corsair jumped over the rail from the top catwalk, sword in hand, as he spiralled down toward the B.O.S.S. unit. His blade plunged through the roof of the mech, piercing the cockpit. He flipped a switch inside his basket hilt and revealed the real power of his sword. The gears on the hilt spun to reform into a new configuration. When it was complete, the pommel's blue stone glowed—a piece of Uriel activating. The sword exploded with an immense electrical discharge, sending it downward into the B.O.S.S. unit, until every electrical system shorted out, killing the pilot and engineer. His rubber-soled boots saved Corsair from electrocution.

One of the Pinkertons aimed at Corsair, but Moon Crow, who was up on the catwalk, stopped him. His Winchester blew the gun right out of the Pinkerton's hand. He dropped to his knees, clenching his hand in pain as his gaping wound bled out. Kiki jumped out and laid her sword across his throat, ready to silence him for good.

'Wait a minute, Kiki,' Corsair commended, stopping her in

her tracks. 'We need him alive.'

He pulled out his sword and jumped off the B.O.S.S. unit, careful not to slip on the hydraulic fluid that was still seeping out of the mech. Corsair walked up to the whimpering prisoner, adding his blade with Kiki's. The Pinkerton, who was clutching the wound on his hand, looked closely at the two edges pointing at him.

'Now then, unless you want to end up like your friends, you better start talking,' Corsair insisted. 'Where is the piece of Uriel?'

He trembled violently, uncertainty growing in his eyes. He decided on the latter.

'It's inside the unit,' he whimpered, nodding his head toward the inactive mech.

Corsair pulled out a handkerchief from his breast pocket and handed it to the injured Pinkerton.

'You better wrap that tightly, or you'll bleed to death,' he consoled.

He quickly grabbed the cloth and wrapped it around his injured hand to stem the bleeding. Corsair walked over to the B.O.S.S. to see if what he said was true.

'Do you believe him?' Kiki asked.

Corsair flipped his sword around, with the blade pointing down to the floor, holding the hilt in his hand. He placed his thumb on the pommel, flipping another switch as the gears on his hilt started moving again.

'We'll soon find out,' he cautioned as the gears finished their alignment.

The gem glowed and emitted a soft light over the mechanical soldier. It moved up and down in a straight line, slowly examining the structure. It stopped just below the cockpit and paused as if the two pieces of the same puzzle found each other.

'It's nice to see *Signore* Tesla's device work, so *meraviglioso!*' Dash complimented, blowing a kiss with his fingers.

Corsair thought about what Dash said before he sheathed his sword.

'Cut her open, Kiki!' he ordered.

As Kiki stepped forward, he lowered his goggles and adjusted the lenses. Her katana, like Corsair's cutlass, had a secret all of its own. She twisted the outer ring of the guard until it clicked, popping open two small valves on either side of the blade collar. A spray of blue flame immediately spread up the sword, sheathing it in a hot corona.

Kiki plunged the blade into the cockpit, carving a hole as if her sword was a super-heated acetylene torch. Corsair watched intently as he casually tapped the side of his goggles to a melodic beat.

'Not to worry, boys, we'll have this sardine can open shortly,' Kiki cajoled.

Once she finished, the steel panel fell open, rattling off the deck. Steam rushed out along with a powerful smell of charred flesh. The smell of death never bothered Corsair. In all his years of pirating, he became used to it.

Corsair reached under the pilot's seat and pulled out a locked strongbox. The steel container was the size of a shoebox with a hinged lid. It had a large padlock securing it shut. He carefully set it down on top of a crate, trying to keep it level.

'Dash, open it!' he asked his best lock picker.

Dash knew just what he needed for the job. He pulled out what appeared to be a cigarette from his shirt pocket and put it in his mouth before striking a match nonchalantly off Knox's armour. He lit the "cigarette" but didn't inhale like you usually would. Instead, he just let it burn slowly before placing the lit end into the locking mechanism. Within seconds, a small "pop" of an explosion burst open the lock.

'It is easy for a *genio* like me!' he boasted.

Knox pulled him back so Corsair could get into the box. He pulled the lock off and opened the lid slowly as a soft, blue glow radiated from inside. It was something truly amazing to see, even for Corsair. Inside a glass cylinder, sealed on both ends by metal caps, was the largest piece of Uriel's comet that he ever laid his eyes on before. It was suspended inside the glass tube by a magnetic field generated between the metal caps on the ends. He picked up the glass container in his hand and looked at the glowing meteorite in awe. Everyone else was equally amazed by the size of the mineral.

'*Lieber Gott*, that's got to be at least three to five kilograms,' Knox exclaimed.

'That's enough power to run the *Galeru* for a thousand years,' Kiki blurted out. 'It's amazing!'

'It's bait,' Corsair stated plainly, 'And we've just walked into a trap!' He carefully put the fragment back into the box and closed the lid, tucking it under his arm. 'We need to get back to the ship now!'

But before they could move, they heard footsteps rushing into the upper catwalks. When they looked up, the ship's security was quickly filing into position with some of the Pinkertons mixed into their ranks. They surrounded them from above, aiming their weapons down at the pirates, ready to fire.

Everyone looked up at more than fifty guns aimed at them.

Kiki couldn't believe the number of armed security personnel standing up there. There were more than double the standard complement for a *Valiant* zeppelin.

'Where did all these goons come from?' Kiki asked.

'They were acting as passengers to confuse our scans with the R.F.M.,' Corsair surmised. 'This whole set up was a trap, specifically for us.'

The sound of a single person clapping their hands echoed in the cargo hold. Corsair looked up and waited to see who led the applause, and he recognised him immediately.

Clapping his hands with a sarcastic smirk to match his glee, he strolled out onto the catwalk. His bright red hair and stark white skin earned him the nickname "The Red Ghost," attributed to his appearance and brutal methods of getting things done. He worked his way up through ERP, keeping workers in line, breaking up strikes, and bullying corporate bosses to giving into ERP's demands during tense negotiations. He wore a bowler hat on his head, a fine dress suit befitting a man of his stature, and carried a shillelagh under his arm. His name was Daniel McTavish, director of ERP Security.

'Well done, me boyo, but you figured it out a little too late,' he jeered. 'I guess you're not as smart as people say you are, eh Corsair?'

'Oh, I don't know "Duke"… the smart thing wouldn't have been letting me get to Kruesi, stealing his thinking machine, or taking down a B.O.S.S. unit,' Corsair sassed back, calling McTavish another nickname he despised.

He was sometimes called "Duke" because of his penchant for fighting, always wanting to duke it out with others. He hated that nickname because it reminded him of his past and many failures.

'This little venture of yours is going to cost ERP a lot of money, and for what, Duke?'

'For that,' McTavish said, pointing at Corsair's blade. 'Your sword!'

Corsair couldn't help but laugh.

'What, with all the brains working for Edison, he still can't figure out how to accurately track down pieces of Uriel? Really? Tesla worked that problem out a long time ago.'

McTavish hated his boss being insulted by a common thief like Corsair. He held Edison in the highest regards with nothing but respect, and this banter of his ticked him off. Yet still, McTavish smiled, thinking he had the upper hand.

'I wouldn't worry about that too much since I'll be prying that sword from your dead hands,' he bragged as the men cocked their weapons to open fire.

In an instant, Dash pulled a bomb out of his pack and slapped it on the box containing Uriel's fragment, holding the plunger in his hand. McTavish's smile went to a frown as he held up his hands, stopping the security forces from firing down into the hold.

'Ah, see, Duke, you're a lot smarter than you look,' Corsair said, countering his insult. 'And by the way, Dash here's got a hair-trigger finger, so don't try anything stupid. Now I figure that this bomb, combined with this fragment's power, will blow this entire ship to pieces. That includes Kruesi, the passengers, these men, and of course, your sorry ass.'

'You'll be dead too, mate. Don't forget that,' McTavish snapped back.

'I'm not worried about my death, Duke. Every day, I meet

more and more like me, ready to fight back against ERP and any other corporation that is willing to kill for its profit,' Corsair extolled. 'The day of the corporate ruler is over; the day of the freedom fighter is coming anew, and there's nothing a bully like you can do to stop it.'

McTavish thought he had the upper hand over these pirates. Having to stand there and endure insults and bravado by these brigands made his blood boil. However, he was more concerned if this intricate plan of his fell apart.

'I tell you what, me boyo. Why don't we settle this man to man?' McTavish countered. 'If you beat me, you get to walk out of here with that piece of Uriel and your lives. If I win, you surrender. Pure and simple.'

Corsair had the face of a champion poker player as he stared down McTavish. He thought for a moment, not saying a word, as if he was even considering the offer.

'Come on, boy, what do you say?' he shouted down as his anger got the best of him. 'You either fight me or blow us all to hell. Which is it?'

'Plan C...' Corsair retorted.

His answer confused McTavish. The head of security started laughing, thinking the pirate had gone mad.

'What the hell is Plan C?' he asked, and as if on cue, the answer came down through the ceiling.

A single drop tube broke through into the cargo hold. They rarely extend down this far. It pierced the superstructure and ripped through one of the helium bladders. It was so powerful, there was no way to seal the opening behind it as helium poured into the cargo hold.

The downdraught choked out the men on the catwalk as

McTavish could only stand there and watch the pirates squeeze into their boarding elevator. Knox had to leave his Gatling gun and ammunition backpack behind to make enough room for all five of them. Kiki was the most uncomfortable, having to get in tight quarters with four men.

The Irish bully was so enraged, he reached into his coat and drew his own Colt M1900.

'I wouldn't do that if I were you,' Corsair warned before he could squeeze the trigger. 'There's enough helium in here to blow us all to bits. Now, I know you don't want to kill Edison's best friend, do you?'

McTavish thought about it before he holstered his weapon.

'Next time, Corsair, your *arse* is mine!'

Corsair just smiled and saluted as he got in the elevator, just as the door shut. As quickly as it came in, the drop tube retracted back through the zeppelin and returned to the *Galeru*. In an instant, the pirates were gone.

McTavish stood there, boiling as he just stared at the empty ceiling.

'Sir!' one of the Pinkerton's yelled at him. 'We have to evacuate and seal the cargo hold, or the helium will suffocate us!'

McTavish nodded his head before he spun on his heels and stormed out of the cargo hold. He lost this battle, but he would win the war.

*

With a loud bang, the drop tube finally retracted into the hangar of the *Galeru*. The overextension tore the canvas and bent the metal ribbing out of shape. Bronx did his best to get the system under control, with hydraulic fluid bursting out from the pipes until he could finally close the hatch and open the door. Kiki was the first one out, pushing her way past Corsair and the others.

'Oh my God, never again!' she screamed after being locked inside the elevator with four men. 'And one of you is in desperate need of a bath!'

Knox and Dash sniffed their armpits to see if it was either of them that offended her.

'Sorry, Kiki, but we needed to get out of there in one piece,' Corsair clarified. 'By the way, Bronx, glad you got my signal. That relay transmitter you put in my goggles worked perfectly.'

'Eager's one to thank, captain. He heard your signal on the bridge and told us you were in trouble. The hard part was overriding the drop tube system to go that far into the *Valiant*.'

'Well, in any case, nice job in getting the tube down to us,' he complimented his engineer with a pat on the back. 'We'd be dead if it wasn't for you.'

'Don't thank me yet, captain. I overloaded the system to send one tube down to the cargo hold,' Bronx explained, wiping the hydraulic fluid off his hands. 'We won't be boarding anyone until I can get this fixed.'

'Well, make a supply list, and we'll send it on to Odysseus Station. Hopefully, they'll have everything there before our arrival.'

'Don't forget a new Gatling gun and ammunition,' Knox added with a glint of sadness in his eyes. '*Brunhilde* was a goddess in my hands. I hated to leave her there.'

'*Brunhilde?*' Bronx queried.

'He names his weapons after Valkyries,' Dash explained. 'He is such a *romantico*!'

'*Brunhilde* did her job,' Knox interjected. 'I just hated to leave her behind.'

'Well, it was worth it, Knox,' Corsair said as he handed the box with the piece of Uriel to Kiki. 'Let's get this locked away for now. I'm sure Tesla will pay us handsomely for this; enough for supplies, repairs, and a little something extra for everyone.'

The crew was happy to hear that. They cheered about the payday awaiting them, but not everyone was delighted.

'I wouldn't be celebrating yet, Corsair, dear,' Fox interrupted. 'While Bronx was handling your rescue, he left me to review the data in Kruesi's little toy.'

'You know how to work a Hollerith Thinking Machine?' Kiki perplexed.

Fox just smiled at her counterpart, loving every minute of this delicious moment.

'I have a great many talents, Kiki. I just don't show all of my cards at once,' she cooed. 'But in reality, all I did was finish loading the punch cards through the infernal contraption and wait for the final result to display on the screen... And it's not good. To make their Cobalt High Energy weapons work properly, they need a pure source of Uriel, an untainted fragment of the comet.'

'Untainted, but aren't they all pure pieces of the comet, *Cara Signora*?' Dash wondered.

'The way Mr Tesla explained it to me was when the pieces of Uriel pass through our atmosphere, it burns away the outer shell protecting the core inside,' Bronx pointed out. 'The core gets exposed to the electromagnetic radiation that protects our atmosphere, altering the structure of the mineral.'

'English, Bronx, not all of us have your Vernian-level

intellect,' Kiki countered.

'It means that the majority of the pieces of Uriel that fall to Earth are no longer pure,' Corsair jumped in. 'They're tainted by our planet. They're looking for pieces still encased in the meteorite shell...' He paused for a moment as things became more evident. 'They need a better way to look for pieces of the comet. Edison wanted to combine his detector with one of Tesla's. That's why they wanted my sword!'

Everyone was shocked as they all realised the truth behind their assault on the Valiant, but one question remained.

'But *Kapitän*, where do we find such a meteorite?' Knox questioned. 'Can such a piece even exist?'

Before Corsair could reply, another voice chimed in out of nowhere.

'It does,' Moon Crow said, speaking up for the first time, surprising everyone as they turned to look at their Apache companion. 'In my home, the great Apache Chief, Geronimo, found a piece of the stone sent from the Creator to bring light to my people. He hid the stone so the Fox could not steal it, returning the fire to the sky.'

'The Fox?' Scarlett said with a smile.

'Not you, Scarlett. The trickster who steals from the Apache all that the Creator gave to his promised people,' Moon Crow explained. 'The Apache sees the piece of Uriel as a gift from *Usen*.'

'And do you know where it is, Moon Crow?' Corsair asked.

'Yes, Captain, I do...'

*

Corsair and The Sky Pirates

London Air Park on the south-eastern edge of Feltham… It took hours for the *Valiant* crew to repair the damage caused by pirates. Even with one bladder gone, the zeppelin was able to stay airborne long enough to finish its journey to Great Britain. The *Valiant* landed at a grass airfield in Hanworth Park House near London. The ground crew conducted the airship landing procedure with precision and accuracy that befitted the White Star line.

Standing at the edge of the airfield, waiting patiently for the zeppelin to begin disembarking passengers, was the man at the top of ERP… Thomas Alva Edison. A worried look caused his brow to furl under his grey hair. Here was a man, an inventor, a genius by all rights, with more than one thousand patents to his name. He was also an industrialist and a capitalist. He never let other competitors get in the way of progress.

Tesla made one of the most significant discoveries in the world when he harnessed the power of Uriel's fragments, but in Edison's point of view, he had no vision of the future. To Edison, the comet's power meant global power, controlling everything to bring about order and peace. That's what he intended to do, by any means necessary.

The first to disembark from the *Valiant* was Kruesi, followed immediately by McTavish and the surviving men from their Pinkerton security detail. Kruesi didn't look as worried as McTavish over the debacle in dealing with Corsair and his Sky Pirates. He reached out and shook Edison by the hand.

'Everything went according to plan, Thomas,' Kruesi extolled.

This revelation surprised McTavish to no end.

'What? Are you daft? They chewed us up and spat us out! It was nothing remotely to the plan I laid out!' he screamed.

'Not your plan, Mr McTavish, but mine,' Edison interrupted.

'I knew that someone of Corsair's ingenuity would see through your charade. So, I reworked it, as it were, to ensure our victory.'

McTavish was shocked that there was another plan in play besides his. It bothered him that Edison didn't trust him enough to let him in on it.

'Oh, don't look so gloomy, Daniel. I didn't tell you about the changes because I didn't want to take a chance that Corsair would figure things out. Let's face it; you're a bad liar.'

McTavish knew his boss was right, and he had a bit of a laugh at his own expense.

'But what about the fragment and the thinking machine?' McTavish asked. 'Corsair, and now probably Tesla, know what we're looking for!'

'That fragment was a small price to pay,' Edison explained as he turned to walk back to his automobile with Kruesi and McTavish following close behind. 'The canister the fragment is in has a small transmitter John designed himself. It will allow us to track that accursed pirate ship from one end of the globe to the other. As for the data, it will only give them a small clue as to our ultimate goal,' Edison continued. 'In the end, Corsair and his crew will lead us to the piece of Uriel we need to finish our research. Once it's in our hands, no one will stop me from achieving my dream of a world utopia... Peace without war... A one world government under the control of those destined to lead.'

Edison got into his car with Kruesi before leaning out to give McTavish one final order.

'Daniel, get your best men together,' he commended. 'And contact Mata Hari in Paris... We need a Shade of her calibre to keep tabs on Corsair.'

With those last instructions, Edison left the airfield. McTavish just smiled, knowing that Edison was on top of things. The hunt was on.

Reviews are the most powerful tools for a publisher and an author. They help to gain attention for the books you enjoy reading. Honest reviews of our books helps to bring them to the attention of other readers.

If you have enjoyed this book, or any of our other books, we would be very grateful if you could spend just five minutes leaving a review. These reviews can be as short or as long as you like.

Other Crystal Peake Anthologies

Traditional stories and beliefs are where folklores begin. Passed through the generations of storytellers, through word of mouth. These ten stories are based on those traditional folklore stories, passed down to our authors. These are their stories to tell, beautifully pieced together for our enjoyment.

A forgotten world of floating islands are the home of their own legendary heroes. A collection of tales set in the same fantastical world about the same magical races. From the demonic elves of the Slay Waterway to the Making of the High Wilds. Are you ready to hear the Tales of the Forgotten World?

Music is a journey, and they're lost in the lyrics.

When musicians Matty and Sandy crack open a dusty old book of folk songs, they hope to escape into the whimsical stylings of the past. They don't expect to actually be taken there.

Yet just a few notes sung from its cursed pages whisks them away to the world of Old England and all its hey-nonny-nonnies, myths and magic. In a dire twist of fate, Sandy is taken prisoner by the heartbroken Lord Donald who seeks to sacrifice her in the hope of resurrecting his lost love.

Knowing he must find Sandy and stop the murderous Lord before May Day, Matty needs allies now more than ever. Can a lustful witch and a plucky swordswoman guide him through the musically-induced mayhem of this strange - yet oddly familiar - world? Or is Sandy well and truly folked?

Drake Banks is a 12-year-old boy who is used to moving from one army camp to another. After the death of his father, Drake and his mother have to get used to living a normal life in the town where she grew up. This proves challenging for Drake as he misses the army life. Drake finds an old arcade in his new town. He loves video games! One day, after arriving at the arcade, Drake discovers a new game called Death Trap. He did not know how his life was about to drastically change. After pressing Start, Drake is sucked into the video game.

Upon entering this new world, Drake has to face a series of dangerous challenges and survive if he wants to get back home. But he soon realises that he is not alone. There are two other competitors, Scott Vent and Crystal Moon, who are computer programmes. The race is on! However, it isn't long before they realise that they cannot face these challenges alone. Can they put their differences aside and work together?

MURDER THE MARCH HARE

H. LYALL

CRYSTAL PEAKS

Cosmo knows he's crazy, his homicidal squirrel tells him so every day. Not that Bandit has to, he just likes reminding him of the facts of the situation. After living at Wellspring Hospital for the last two years not much has changed for Cosmo. His pills are still rainbow coloured, therapy is still a bore, and above all he isn't getting better. Bandit's trying to help too, but the dead body he brought in seems to be causing problems. In an attempt to understand what's going on behind the secure walls a band of misfits come together in the search for a murderer. However, it's easier said than done when you don't know what's real. Maybe it's easier? Maybe, just maybe, the only people who can find the truth are those that have to question everything.

AIR FAY

Lost... in a world she doesn't recognize.

Trapped... without a clue who she is.

Aria woke up in a forest that defies imagination, unsure of who she was or how she got there. Guided by a runaway stranger, she delves into the mystical plane where fairies are real and magic exists.

But in this enchanting land of beauty, darkness slithers all around...

When the shadows invade her life, Aria's only hope of making it out alive is to channel a strength within her she never knew existed. Finding herself thrust into the middle of a siege that could destroy the realm, Aria is faced with the choice to retreat back to the life she once knew or stand and fight with her newfound friends.

Will she sacrifice her human life to join the fae? Or can she find a way to embrace all that she is, and rise as an unlikely heroine with the power to save two worlds from annihilation?